The Mayor of Heaven

Also by Lynn Kanter

On Lill Street

The Mayor of Heaven

by

Lynn Kanter

Third Side Press

Chicago, Illinois

Copyright © 1998 by Lynn Kanter

Author's note: While there is a town in New York state called Sterling, the town of Sterling, New York described in this novel is fictional.

Cover art copyright © 1997 by Rhonda Tullis
Book design and production by Midge Stocker

Printed on recycled, acid-free paper in the United States of America.

Library of Congress Cataloging-in-Publication Data

Kanter, Lynn, 1954-
    The mayor of Heaven / by Lynn Kanter. —1st ed.
      p. cm.
    ISBN 1-879427-29-x (acid-free paper).—ISBN 1-879427-30-3 (pbk.: acid-free paper)
    I. Title.
  PS3561.A49M38 1997
  813.54—dc21   97-7030
                                 CIP

Third Side Press, Inc.
2250 W. Farragut
Chicago, IL 60625-1863
773-271-3029
ThirdSide@aol.com

First edition, October 1997
10 9 8 7 6 5 4 3 2 1

DEDICATION

For Janet

FOREWORD

by Susan Hester

The Mayor of Heaven is a work of fiction written by Lynn Kanter, who is one of my closest friends. I knew Lynn before I met my life partner, Mary-Helen Mautner. And Lynn knew me through the years when Mary-Helen had breast cancer and died.

So when I tell people about Lynn's new book, they ask me, "Is this your story?" And I reply, "This is all of our stories." The novel does not tell my story in the plot or the details. But it is my story, as it is the story of *every* family of friends who has lived through the process of losing one of our own, someone we never imagined being without.

As I read this book, I was taken back to my own experience of Mary-Helen's life, dying, and death. I cried with the old pent-up tears that collect in me over time and then come roaring out. And as I read, I nodded with knowing, sighed at the familiar, laughed out loud, and cried some more.

The Mayor of Heaven shows us a year in the lives of four friends—not just any year, but their first year without Claire. I liked these characters and was glad to get to know them—the partner, the best lesbian friend, the best straight friend, and the best man friend—brought together by their love for Claire, who has been dead for 6 months when the book begins.

Claire's partner Lucy is for me a true character, because her pain is so thorough and she refuses to be rushed through it, refuses to "get on with it" to make things easier for those around her. The other three friends experience the paradox of learning that as a person dies and gives us a bottomless loss, she also gives us gifts, depending on what we need, what shields need to be broken through, how we are to be freed to enter more fully into own lives through witnessing the death of a friend.

If you have been there as a partner or a friend, you will think some of the pages of *The Mayor of Heaven* were taken right from your own life. Some of the pages you will be glad you were spared. I was relieved that this novel is not a fairy tale. It does not have an ending that will give you instant relief, but it will leave you with a taste of life that makes you know your own story is universal.

So many times since Mary-Helen died, people have said to me, "I can't imagine what it's like to lose a partner," or "When my friend was sick I didn't know what to say or do." If you read this book, it will help you know how to be loyal, what you can give, how you can help, and when you can't.

Pay attention to the scene where Aunt Estelle calls late at night and asks the right questions and tells the best stories. Pay attention to these characters, and promise yourself to know better what to do the next time you have an opportunity to be part of the transition we all will one day make. Read this book and figure out how you could be as true as these four friends, as ready to change your own life for a friend who is losing hers.

Read this book for pleasure, live or relive the pain, read it and be instructed by it, read it and enjoy it as a book you can't put down. Follow the examples and you will open up, you will grieve without time limits, you will know how to live in solidarity with those in pain around you, how to give to them, how to take from them, and how to let them be.

I know this novel was not meant to be a "how-to" book. Yet we have to rely on books like *The Mayor of Heaven* as instruction manuals, because none of this is taught anywhere, and we don't talk about it enough, despite the fact that this story happens to all of us. Read this book and know it is fiction—true to life.

—SUSAN HESTER
Founder, Mary-Helen Mautner Project for Lesbians with Cancer

Susan Hester is the founder of the Mary-Helen Mautner Project for Lesbians with Cancer, in Washington, DC. The Mautner Project provides direct services to lesbians with cancer and their partners and caregivers; educates the lesbian community about cancer issues, and the health care community about the special concerns of lesbians; and conducts public policy advocacy on behalf of lesbian health issues. Susan Hester is also a cofounder of the National Breast Cancer Coalition and the National Coalition of Feminist and Lesbian Cancer Projects.

ACKNOWLEDGMENTS

I want to thank some of the people who have assisted, supported, and inspired me through the long process of writing this novel:

Midge Stocker, editor, publisher, and founder of Third Side Press, for her courage and commitment to lesbian literature.

The women of the Feminist Women's Writing Workshops, who create for one week each summer the ideal atmosphere for enlarging writing skills and spirit.

My employer, the Center for Community Change, for enabling me to attend the Workshops.

The talented writers who commented on the novel during its development, particularly Joan Dickenson, Mickie Grover, Cindy Lollar, and Maida Tilchen.

The perceptive readers who shared their insights with me, including Charlene Sinclair, Deb Morris, Susan Hester, and my favorite in-house editor, Janet Coleman.

And for the lessons they taught, Mary-Helen Mautner, Mary Grace Sinnott, Jeffrey Atkinson, Rasheda Wallace, Ann Timmerman, Helen Boscoe, and the women who loved them.

∞ ∞ ∞ 1 ∞ ∞ ∞

HAIRCUT

Lucy found it hard to believe that despite everything, here she was, getting her hair cut.

Glossy, straight, dark brown, so baby-fine it flew up in alarm at the first hint of static electricity, her hair took forever to grow. When Lucy was a teenager, she could never get it long enough to be fashionable. So she had settled early-on for the style she wore today: shoulder length, acceding to a natural part over her left eyebrow, tucked behind her ears or held back from her face with some funky device Claire used to find. Filigreed silver combs. Minnie Mouse barrettes. Ceramic butterflies alight on bobby pins.

Now her wet hair dampened her shoulders, and Lucy sank into the familiar black swivel chair. Twice a year she came to the Blue Shampoo for a trim. She had skipped her last appointment, which reminded her, as if she needed reminding, that Claire had been in the ground 6 months.

Holly, their hairdresser—Lucy's hairdresser—wrapped a blue flowered smock around her. Lucy felt Holly watching, but she didn't look up.

"How're you holding up?" asked Holly in her high, light voice.

Underneath the smock, Lucy's fists clenched in her lap. She stared at them through the fabric. "Okay," she mumbled. "Thanks." Her eyes stung; each flower trembled and sprouted a twin. Holly squeezed her shoulder. She picked up the comb and they were both relieved.

Generally a chatterbox, today Holly was silent. The click of her scissors made the only conversation as she combed and trimmed. Lucy didn't mind; she had that effect on everyone these days. Perhaps grief *was* contagious, as people seemed to fear.

Lucy had expected bereavement to feel like a long sadness. Instead she discovered grief was a new form of gravity that weighted her bones and turned the very air heavy.

She glanced in the mirror. Tall, thin, breezy, Holly was barely older than the college students Lucy taught. Today her short curls gleamed a bright, carroty red, a spectrum away from the prim chestnut she was trying out the last time Lucy had seen her—a lifetime ago, in the great world of Before.

Lucy knew she could cheer her up by talking about the aerobics class Holly led, or by asking about her husband, Todd. But Lucy didn't ask. She didn't have the energy. She had only one question for Holly, and she liked her too much to mention it: Is it true that people's hair continues to grow after they're dead?

Lucy had wanted Claire to be cremated. No more deterioration, no more decay. Just the flash, the fire, then soothing, silent ash. But Claire wouldn't have it.

"It reminds me of Auschwitz," she had said, as she sat surrounded by a wall of white pillows in the rented hospital bed that had replaced their own. She wore a red sweatshirt that accentuated her pallor; her fuzzy scalp was hidden by a jaunty lavender baseball cap. Lucy was surprised Claire did not realize how strongly her sunken black eyes and sepulchral cheeks already called that era to mind.

Standing at the tall mullioned window beside the bed, Lucy watched the snow fall—dry, distinct flakes that settled into cushiony folds and draped down the sloping street. She could see neighbors shoveling their driveways, pulling a child on a bright blue sled, casting arcs of sand on the path to the mailbox. It all seemed as distant and remarkable as normal life.

Inside their saltbox house, with its thick walls and canted roof, summer reigned. With pounding labor, the aging furnace kept the temperature hovering at around 80°. Claire could never get warm enough, while Lucy, in her shorts and t-shirt, was sweating.

"And what would you do with the ashes?" Claire demanded. "I don't want to be in a mayonnaise jar on your next girlfriend's mantel."

Lucy folded her arms against her chest to keep from clutching Claire's blue-tipped fingers. "It would have to be a pickle jar," she replied. "You know I don't like mayonnaise." Familiar as Lucy was with the tone of these exchanges, it horrified her to her soul. How could they even be speaking about these things— Claire's death! the disposition of her body!—much less joking about them? But Claire insisted on it. The gallows humor made it easier, maybe even possible, to discuss some of the things they had to face.

"And I don't like pickles," Claire countered. "Another good point in favor of burial." She pulled the blue comforter up to her chest and spoke more quietly. "It sounds kind of peaceful, doesn't it? To rest in the ground? And Lucy, I'm tired."

"I know, sweetheart."

"Besides," Claire continued, "I've always wanted a place in the country. You know, a tomb of one's own."

∞ ∞ ∞

Lucy had first seen that flash of black humor the night they met, more than thirteen years before. They were both living in Albany, both perched between permanence and flight, staying in furnished apartments in shabby neighborhoods. Lucy was an adjunct professor with a year's contract to teach literature to undergrads at the State University of New York. Claire was in town to edit a series of programs for the local public television station.

Lucy spent much of her time that year in the spacious kitchen of a ramshackle house rented by her friend Jane McKay. She too worked at SUNY, coordinating services for the university's deaf students. On that particular afternoon they were lolling at Jane's long wooden table, elbows planted amidst the cheerful clutter of notebooks, file boxes, pencils, and mugs of tea. Jane was flipping through her index cards. Lucy was whining.

"Why can't I meet a woman in this town?" she demanded. "I don't need to find the love of my life. I just want some adult company and maybe a dash of romance."

Jane didn't look up. In fact, it seemed as though she were regarding Lucy from the top of her head, where her glasses balanced on her wavy blonde hair. "If I found you even remotely attractive, this conversation would be very discouraging."

Lucy laughed. "Oh, Jane, you know I love you—"

"—only not in that way," they finished in unison.

"All right." Jane shook a handful of index cards into order and smacked them on the table. "I know only one woman in Albany who's not a nun, in a couple, or straight. Her name is Claire Morganstern. She's tall, she's talkative, she's opinionated, and she's my oldest friend."

"Is she cute?"

"Naturally."

"Great! Introduce us. Why have you been holding out on me?"

"I harbored the strange notion that you could find your own women." Jane had light blue eyes that tended to disappear when she laughed. But her eyes did not crinkle into amusement; they fixed Lucy with a solemn stare. "Now, if I introduce you to Claire, you have to promise not to break her heart or tame her spirit. And for God's sake, don't fall in love."

"Why not?"

"Just don't."

"But why? You can't state that like some biblical injunction. Give me one good reason."

"For one thing, neither one of you has any idea where you'll be living a year from now. Chances are good it won't be in the same town."

"What else?"

"Self-interest. I don't want the two of you disappearing into some love cocoon, leaving me alone with the world's most disorganized dissertation." Jane's eloquent hands fluttered in the air.

"So tell me about your friend," Lucy cajoled. "What does she do?"

"She's in TV."

"What channel? Have I seen her?"

"I said she's *in* TV, not *on* it. She's an editor, one of those behind-the-scenes people. Anyway, we grew up together in Glens Falls."

"What's she doing in Albany?"

Jane reached for her cards. "Look, I'll talk to Claire tonight. If she's interested she'll call you, and you can grill her yourself."

Claire did call, and they had one of those lighthearted, exploratory conversations that could suggest either a compatible connection or that they had used up all their charm on the phone. They arranged a date, and Lucy's heart fluttered appropriately when Claire stepped into the living room to pick her up.

She had dark, heavy-lidded, liquid eyes. She had wild, black curly hair. She had long, strong-looking legs. Did she also have a microscopic cell of cancer growing in her left breast even then?

They buckled themselves into Claire's car with all the trepidation and promise of a first date, heading for one of Albany's trendier restaurants. But they never made it. At the stop light two blocks from Lucy's apartment, a man smashed the back window with a baseball bat, grabbed Claire's leather briefcase from the back seat, and dashed away into the dusk before they could register what had happened.

By the time they fumbled open their seatbelts and leaped out of the car, he was gone. The two women stood there, staring after him amidst the honking horns and flying curses of the other drivers who swerved around them to squeal through the intersection. Finally Claire turned to Lucy, grinned across the roof of her car, and asked, "How are you enjoying the date so far?"

It was hopeless, they knew, but they drove to a police station to report the incident. Neither one had seen the man except as a fleeing figure dressed in a dark parka and ski cap. Besides, his particular crime was so popular it had its own name: the smash 'n' grab. But it was a rented car, and Claire would need the police report when she made her insurance claim.

They sat on tan plastic chairs bolted to the tan linoleum floor of the police station. The grimy outer room was deserted except for one blond crewcut cop who leaned behind a high wooden desk. From double doors to the right came the murmur of male voices. Lucy studied the cop covertly as Claire bent over her clipboard. He had the young, truculent face of a football player. What did he make of them, two thirtyish women in their trim jeans, their leather boots, their down jackets? Could he spot them instantly as a couple of lesbians? The thought made Lucy smile.

"What were you grinning about in the police station?" Claire asked later. They were lingering over coffee and pie in the diner they had decided was the most fitting destination after the evening's adventure. "I think you made that little cop nervous."

"I was just wondering how dykey we looked. Besides, you should talk. Someone robs you, and you start cracking jokes."

"I'm on a date, I'm trying to make a good impression, and some guy makes off with my briefcase. It just struck me as funny, that's all."

"Well, I would have been upset. I *was* upset, and it wasn't even my briefcase."

Claire lifted one shoulder in a shrug. "What did he take? A hunk of leather. My wallet was in my coat pocket. My keys were in the ignition. He got a bunch of tape logs and some pens. Maybe my favorite highlighter. But hey, he didn't smash 'n' grab us."

"True." Lucy laughed. "But in a sense, he stole your time. Won't you have to redo the work he took?"

"Maybe a little. I've got copies of most of it back at the station."

"Does that mean you're a cautious person?"

Claire tilted her head; rows of little wrinkles appeared on her forehead. "In real life, no, I don't think so. But in my work, I'm very careful." She leaned across the speckled Formica table, and Lucy felt her heart sway. "I mean, think about it sometime when you're watching TV. Every minute of programming is made up of 60 seconds. And every second of videotape is made up of 30 frames. That's 30 chances a second to get something wrong. So I'm careful." Claire smiled. "But what about you, Lucy? Are you cautious?"

"Not at all."

"So you're daring?"

"No . . . more like haphazard. For example, I moved to Albany without having any place to live. Just packed up the car and drove. I felt sure I'd find an apartment right away, and I did. Somehow I've always had this absurd conviction that I'll land on my feet."

"A survivor," Claire had nodded on that cold spring evening so many years ago. "I like that."

∞ ∞ ∞

And apparently she was right, because here was Lucy at the Blue Shampoo, getting herself prettied up for tonight's gathering. Claire was gone, she was gone forever, and Lucy was getting her hair cut. So it seemed Lucy had survived, although for what reason, she couldn't imagine.

A surge of heartache rocked her, and she lurched in her seat. Holly's long, sharp scissors nipped her earlobe, drawing blood but no pain. Lucy didn't even realize it had happened until she heard the other woman gasp, "Damn!"

Lucy glanced at her left shoulder, where a red blotch was slowly obliterating the blue flowers. She was surprised an earlobe had so much blood. She turned back to the glass to watch the drama.

"Someone get me a clean towel and a bandage," Holly called out. Scissors stilled across the mirrored universe.

So I've been cut, so what? thought Lucy. It was just something that was happening in the mirror. She had no sense of being involved in the incident, of being inside that bleeding body.

"Lucy, I am so sorry," Holly exclaimed. "I've never hurt anyone before."

"Don't worry. It doesn't hurt."

"Well, it will. And to think, I had to cut you, of all people. You've got enough problems."

"Holly, it's okay." Lucy patted her hand. "Don't feel bad. I've always wanted pierced ears."

And Lucy laughed. It sounded rusty and strange but she kept on laughing. Because that was Claire's voice speaking, her words, her intonation, and Lucy hadn't heard them in a long, long time.

∞ ∞ ∞ **2** ∞ ∞ ∞

INSOMNIA

Many people feel that as they grow older, time seems to speed up. Hours, weeks, entire months hurtle past them. Not Harry. His days toiled by in slow motion, each one longer than the day before. There were a number of reasons for this. One of them was the fact that he'd been awake for most of the past year.

His insomnia was prodigious. It resisted relaxation tapes. It rebelled at Valium. It laughed at meditation. As Harry yanked a shopping cart from the tangled wire herd in front of the supermarket, he reflected that his insomnia was the most loyal companion he'd ever known, and no matter where he ran he couldn't escape it.

Like many men, Harry used to fantasize about making love to beautiful women in sunlit bedrooms overlooking the ocean. Now he fantasized about deep, dreamless sleep. Night after night he imagined it in caressing detail: the effortless rhythm of his lungs, the profound relaxation of his limbs, the fluttering eyelids of REM giving way to the unconscious miracle of sleep.

But nothing—not sex or drugs or rock and roll— could help Harry achieve this sleep. And it was all Claire's fault.

∞ ∞ ∞

Claire had been his best friend. They had met in college, when they were both scared 17-year-olds from small towns, let loose for the first time on the cold, clean, crowded Albany campus of the State University of New York.

Claire was tall, big-boned, with a heart-shaped face and coils of black hair cascading down her back. She wore her jeans slung low across her hips. She never stopped talking. The only way to shut her up was to make her laugh, which Harry did as often as possible. She had one of those silent, helpless laughs. It cracked him up every time to see this big outspoken woman caught in the grip of her soundless laughter.

When they were in school, Claire still slept with men—a lot of men. Harry was convinced she was trying to find Mr. Right through the process of elimination. He had reached this conclusion during many late nights spent with Claire, wolfing down Raisin Bran and regaling each other with stories about their conquests. Then, during their senior year, Claire had figured out she was a lesbian, and suddenly her private life became much more private.

Even before that, it had somehow been clear to both of them they were not meant to be lovers. Sometimes they stood side by side and studied themselves in a mirror, sighing theatrically about what a good-looking couple they would have made. Harry's sandy-colored ponytail made a perfect counterpoint to Claire's wild dark curls; his square jaw complemented her pointy, dimpled chin; his blue eyes would meet her dark ones in the watery dorm mirror and make her hiccup with laughter. There was some kind of spark there, all right, but it wasn't romance.

Still, this lesbian business was hard to take. "How can you prefer sleeping with women?" Harry would demand.

"How can you?" Claire would reply.

"I'm supposed to! I'm a man."

"So? Does that mean you should get all the good stuff?"

"Don't start that with me, Claire. This isn't about feminism."

"Isn't it?" she would smile at him. "Okay, Harry, let me put it this way. If you could spend the night next to a soft, rounded, affectionate lover, or a big hairy one with bristly cheeks and a body like wood, which would you choose?"

"That's a ridiculous comparison. Besides, men can be affectionate too."

"True," Claire would admit. "You are. But the fact is, I feel right when I'm with a woman, and you can't talk me out of it."

"I can try."

Harry and Claire played out many variations of this conversation. Each time he hoped the ending would change. Each time he was thwarted. He could not win a fight against Claire's nature, and he knew it.

"Harry," she told him once as they sprawled in front of the extinct fireplace in his off-campus apartment, "one day you'll make some woman a lovely husband."

"So will you, Claire." It was a feeble spring evening, a couple of months before graduation. The weather wasn't quite warm enough to suggest cold beer, but they had downed a few anyway.

"Shut up, Harry, I'm trying to tell you something serious here."

"Okay. What is it?"

"I just hope you'll wait to settle down until your tastes mature. Because some day you might want to turn on the lights and talk to a woman."

Harry considered this. It was true he gravitated toward hot-looking girls with scant intellectual abilities, which probably is what saved him from making a terrible mistake with Claire. "All right," he agreed. "I'll wait."

"Promise me you won't decide to marry anyone until you find yourself mulling over an interesting conversation you had with her."

"Thinking about her bra size isn't good enough?"

Claire kicked him with her round-toed sneaker. "I mean it, Harry. Promise me. Then I won't have to worry about you so much when we leave school."

"I promise."

After graduation Harry left for New York City, where he got a job at a small gray desk in a large blue-chip accounting firm. Claire started her broadcasting career printing cue cards, labeling tapes, and making coffee at a television station outside Scranton, Pennsylvania.

They managed to stay close, talking on the phone and spending occasional weekends together chasing down the most exotic cuisine they could find in New York or whatever town Claire called home during those early wandering years. Then Claire had met Lucy Rogers, and after a couple of years settled down with her in Sterling, a flourishing college town in upstate New York. Harry became such a frequent visitor that he kept clothes in their guest room.

Not long after Claire and Lucy bought their house, Harry spent the entire day helping them scrape generations of paint off the beautiful wood moldings in the living room. "Are you sure you're not gay?" Lucy asked him—not for the first time. The three of them wore matching red bandannas over their hair, which he thought might have prompted Lucy's question.

"Sorry." Harry wiped his hands on his ruined jeans. "But don't worry, I'm not after her ass."

"And why not?" Claire demanded. "Because I'm not as cute as the little blonde nymphets you fancy?"

"No, because I'm scared of your girlfriend." This made Claire dissolve into her silly, silent laughter, because sharp-featured, sweet-natured Lucy was the least intimidating person on earth.

"Just think of us as siblings," Claire counseled her partner. "I always wanted a baby brother, but my parents refused to comply, so I had to find my own."

"Hey, who's the baby here?" he interrupted. "I'm older than you are."

"Chronologically." Claire turned back to Lucy. "You'll get used to him, honey. Everyone does."

As the years passed, Harry was pleased to feel that Lucy grew not only used to him but fond of him. When he had first come up with the idea of fleeing Manhattan for the more livable pace of Sterling, it had been Lucy who encouraged him, while Claire peppered him with questions about what he hoped to find there. He was not following Claire, exactly, but following her example: settling in a place where he could breathe, where he already had a family of sorts. Lucy learned to treat him like a genial brother-in-law who could be counted on to pick them up at the airport or bring over videos and ice cream on lazy Friday nights. In fact, Claire and Harry did grow to be like siblings—twins, almost, because their birthdays were only 3 weeks apart.

For 3 weeks of every year, Harry patronized Claire relentlessly, answering her every challenge with, "You'll understand when you get to be my age." Only now Claire would never be his age, because she was dead. That was why he couldn't sleep.

"It was just the tiniest lump," Lucy told him over and over when Claire was first diagnosed. "It was like a seed. Or a piece of gravel. A raisin." She dropped her head into her hands. "Oh, God, I should have spotted it sooner."

"Lucy, you found it as soon as it was noticeable." Harry tried to comfort her, his arm around her narrow shoulders. "The doctor said by the time a tumor can be felt, the cancer has been in the woman's body for years."

He made the motions, he said the words, but he couldn't convince himself. If Claire were his woman, he sure as hell would have noticed a fucking tumor! How could this be happening? No one gets breast cancer except old ladies, he raged to himself.

It was late June when Claire was diagnosed, Harry recalled, a green, glowing summer day just like today. Six months later she was dead. So swift it was, and so unstoppable. She got sick and died. Got sick and died. Such a simple phrase, hiding a wealth of horror.

Harry found himself murmuring the words aloud as he stared at the armies of lettuce arrayed before him. A woman glanced at him, trundled away behind her rattling grocery cart. Harry didn't blame her. He must look like a lunatic—a tall man, unshaven, talking to himself as he stood rooted in the produce aisle of the valley's busiest supermarket.

There were no supermarkets in the small New York town where Harry grew up. Not far away was a fair-sized grocery store, but Harry's family never shopped there. His mother always took the kids to the Food Mart, only three blocks from their house, where you could get white bread, canned goods, and limp produce 24 hours a day.

The Food Mart was convenient, all right, and like many convenience stores, it sold only the smallest sizes of everything. How many 6-ounce cans of peas does it take to feed a family with 8 children? A lot. Only when he began to manage other people's money for a living did Harry see a connection between his parents' shopping habits and the fact that his family had lived on soup and crackers for the last days of each month.

When he had lived in Manhattan, Harry was thrilled by the profusion of the world's bounty heaped in the crowded, hectic aisles of legendary shops like Zabar's—even the common corner market. Later, when he moved to Sterling, he was dazzled by the long, spacious supermarket shelves gleaming with colorful displays.

"How many brands of cereal does one civilization need?" he had once demanded of Claire as they guided their carts down those endless aisles. "I mean, look at this display. Why would any store carry so many varieties of olives?"

"To entice the palates of over-fed, self-indulgent, white, middle-class aspirants to the good life," she replied. "People like ourselves."

"Well, I like freedom of choice as much as the next guy, but at some point it becomes a burden."

"I'll keep that in mind the next time you complain that they're out of decaf mocha java beans and you have to settle for hazelnut."

But Harry couldn't blame his current paralysis on the overabundance of salad options. He was frozen with dread at the thought of the dinner whose ingredients he was supposed to be selecting.

Tonight Claire's closest friends would gather in her house to talk about life without her. Rasheda, Jane, Harry, and of course Lucy. They would dine at the familiar round table, sip coffee out of handmade mugs, relax after dinner on the frayed couch. Every item in the house told a story about Claire and Lucy, if only the tale of the vanished treasure they had once called daily life. Harry didn't know how Lucy could bear to live there. He could hardly stand the prospect of walking in the door tonight. What did he have to say to these women? To anyone?

They had all lost Claire, but Harry had lost her first. The instant Claire was diagnosed, something within her shifted. She moved beyond him to a shore he couldn't reach no matter how he struggled. It seemed to be a place women could find without effort.

Harry had felt a constant need to be close to her, as if he could keep her safe with his physical strength. But Claire told him she did not want to be touched. Yet time after time he saw her reach for the hand of Lucy or Jane. When he stopped in after work, he would find Claire stretched out on the couch, watching the news, her head in the lap of some woman friend, the visitor's hand casually stroking her forehead.

Harry understood completely. To find solace in the embrace of women was exactly what he himself craved, and sought, and found lacking, and sought again with someone else. But what he craved most of all was to have Claire healthy and restored to him, along with the easy, joking friendship he had relied upon all those years.

They had always laughed about everything; no topic was off limits. Once Claire got sick, her humor became merciless. Harry found himself wincing, winded with the effort of keeping up.

"Oh, don't be so aggressive!" she would some-times chide him, repeating the term her oncologist, Constance Walker, had used to describe her cancer. Or, tossing back a handful of M&Ms, Claire would re-mark, "If white sugar really is a preservative, you don't have to worry about embalming me." Later, when eat-ing was a habit that had passed out of her life, he would remember that moment and marvel.

One fall morning, thumbing through the newspaper, Claire exclaimed, "Look, Harry! We can get a 40-inch TV delivered today and make no payments until next year. Let's buy it! Connie says I probably won't live that long." And she clutched her stomach, not in pain or terror, but shaking with her silent laughter.

Harry laughed with her. But the joke was on him, because deep down he never expected Claire to die. And when she did, shortly before New Year's as Dr. Walker had predicted, he was astonished.

He couldn't believe he would never, ever see Claire again. He couldn't believe that no matter where he looked, he would never find her. He couldn't believe that his beard still grew, that mail still got delivered, that strangers still nattered about everyday things.

Now he had had 6 months to discover how to mourn Claire's loss, and tonight in front of everyone he would have to reveal that he hadn't progressed an inch. Claire's death was the worst thing that had ever happened to Harry, and he had yet to shed a tear.

The others—her women friends—were different. They wept. They sobbed. They "vented their pain," they "shared it," they "got it out." How did they do this? He had no idea.

He was a walking sorrow, and no one noticed. No one understood his deep dry grief.

∞ ∞ ∞ 3 ∞ ∞ ∞

THE LAST AFRO

The sun rose slowly, gilding the sloping roofs of the houses and tinting the velvet hills first charcoal, then mauve, then green. Rasheda Cooper couldn't care less. She sat in the tiny enclosed world of the TV station's announce booth, swinging her feet and playing back memories of Claire.

The booth contained only a chair, a shelf angled to hold copy, and a microphone. Gray tweed carpet covered the floor and shelf; the walls, the ceiling, even the inside of the door were upholstered in thick, gray egg-crate foam. The room was soundproof, with no hard surfaces to deflect an announcer's voice. Claire had likened it to a padded cell. Rasheda called it the womb room.

It was to the womb room she retired whenever she needed to be alone to figure out a work problem or escape the high-stakes pressure of the editing suite. The mystery she pondered now, Rasheda knew, could not be resolved in this brief hour before she returned to the demands of family life and Saturday chores. But tonight she would commemorate the half-year anniversary of Claire's passing, and Rasheda felt she owed herself and her friend this time of reflection. Claire had left this life so quickly Rasheda still could not accept that she was gone.

It had been the same when Claire was sick. Anyone with eyes could see the cancer stealing her away. Yet Rasheda could only believe it for a few seconds at a time before she fell back on her faith that God or medicine or Claire's own stubbornness would save her.

But Lord, those few seconds of recognition.

∞ ∞ ∞

"Over, then under," Rasheda had instructed Claire on an August afternoon almost a year ago. "Over, then under."

The two women sat on Claire's couch, surrounded by colorful squares of silk. Between them slumped a large, soft-bodied doll. Rasheda wrapped a red scarf around the doll's big plastic head and folded it into a tidy turban. "See? Now you make sure it's snug, tuck in this last little tail, and you're there. Instant glamour."

"Even a doll looks good in one of your creations," said Claire.

From the paper bag at her feet, Rasheda drew out a fresh scarf of forest green. "Try it again."

"Okay," Claire muttered. "I'm going to get it this time. And then we're going to practice on me."

"Go ahead." As they leaned together over the doll, heads tilted at the same angle, Rasheda was sharply aware of Claire's waxy gray face and her own brown skin, gleaming with health.

"Why do you wear these things?" Claire demanded, fumbling with the scarf. "You haven't had chemo."

"No, but can you imagine how Gerald would react if I wore my hair like this at work?" Rasheda's hair surrounded her face in a glorious crinkled halo.

"I think he's jealous."

"Kevin tells me, 'I can't believe my wife wears the last Afro in America.' Even my own mama used to say, 'Child, what are you going to do about that head?'"

"So why do you keep it, if it causes you so much grief?"

"Because no one up here knows how to deal with natural hair. When I lived in Washington it was different, but now every time I go into a salon they want to process it or treat it or do some stupid thing to it. But nobody's messin' with my hair. So at work I pull it into a bun or wear these headwraps, and at night I let it go free."

"Well, I think it looks great. And those turbans you wear are very elegant."

"They're headwraps, honey, not turbans."

"Okay, headwraps. And they're still elegant—unlike this." Claire pointed to her own bedraggled effort.

"What do you say we take a break? You look tired."

"Let me try one more time. I think I'm getting the hang of it."

She watched Claire struggle with the slippery cloth, her pale fingers clumsy, the tip of her tongue just visible in the corner of her mouth. Rasheda thought of Claire's hands darting across the editing keyboard and her heart twisted. She remembered their first conversation, which had also been their first fight.

Rasheda had applied for a job as assistant editor at WSTR, Sterling's independent television station. "The ad said 'experience preferred,'" she had fretted that morning to Kevin as he scooped cereal off Keisha's fat little chin and spooned it back into her mouth. Dressed in her best suit, Rasheda sat safely away from the toddler's high chair.

"You have 2 years' experience," Kevin replied in his soothing low voice. "That should count for something."

"Yes, but I was a tape operator. This is an editing job. It's a whole different thing."

"If editing experience was a prerequisite, the ad would have said experience 'necessary,' not 'preferred.' You'll do fine, sugar. They'd be lucky to get you."

Rasheda and Kevin had recently moved to Sterling from Washington, DC. They had been drawn to the town by the good schools and reasonable housing costs as well as by the burgeoning African-American community fed by streams of faculty and graduates from the area's several colleges and universities. In addition, Kevin's family lived not far away in Troy, and the couple was thrilled by the idea of their daughter growing up near her grandparents.

Now Kevin was comfortably ensconced as a junior-high science teacher, and Rasheda was jittery as she waited to be called for her job interview. She sat in the station's reception room eyeing the other applicants, all young white men who were no doubt more highly trained than herself. One of them played a video game as he waited, oblivious to the assault of obnoxious beeps and buzzes on the nerves of his neighbors.

A tall woman with dark curly hair pushed open the door to the reception room. "Rasheda Cooper?"

The woman gave her a brief smile and a strong handshake. "I'm Claire Morganstern." She ushered Rasheda through the door and turned back to the young man with the video game. "Would you mind turning the volume down?" she asked pleasantly.

He shrugged. "There's no volume control."

"Then turn it off," she replied in the same even tone.

As Rasheda followed Claire down a busy hallway and into a small orderly office, she realized this woman was not leading her to meet the senior editor; she *was* the senior editor. Rasheda might just stand a chance after all. Her optimism lasted throughout the interview until Claire said the three deadly words: "Can you type?"

Rasheda gripped the wooden arms of her chair. "The newspaper ad didn't mention typing. It talked about editing. I'm not interested in being someone's secretary."

Claire's heavy eyebrows shot up. "I don't need a secretary. I need an assistant editor. And that job calls for a lot of things, including manual dexterity."

Claire leaned toward Rasheda and transfixed her with her dark, sparkling eyes. "Half the men in that waiting room have more technical experience than you do. My guess is most of them are great at clicking a mouse, but if I sat them at a keyboard they wouldn't know how to use both hands. If you do, that gives you an edge. Because I can teach someone technical skills in half the time it takes to teach hand-eye coordination. So now, Ms. Cooper, if you don't mind telling me, can you type?"

Without blinking, Rasheda answered. "Fifty-five words a minute."

Three years after that nervous morning, Rasheda watched Claire fumble with a scarf. The fabric slipped from Claire's fingers and puddled in her lap. She closed her eyes and let her bony head rest against the back of the couch. Rasheda saw that folding the silk had exhausted her. With a shock of grief, she realized Claire would never work again.

"You know, something just occurred to me," Rasheda said lightly.

Eyes still closed, Claire answered. "What's that?"

"You can mess with these scarves all day, but you'll never get the hang of it. It's an African thang."

Claire smiled. "Are you saying I fold like a white girl?"

"That's right."

"Well, you hug like a straight girl."

"What's that supposed to mean?"

"It means you put your arms on someone's shoulders and give a cautious little squeeze. No holding. No body contact."

"Perhaps this would be a good time to talk about the deep-seated passion for me you've obviously suppressed all these years."

Claire laughed, a silent exhalation of air. "Don't flatter yourself, Rasheda. But pay attention when you say goodbye to Lucy today. You'll see what a real hug is like."

"That doesn't prove anything. For all I know, Lucy has the hots for me too."

With an obvious effort, Claire opened her eyes and turned toward Rasheda. "Lucy could never love a woman like you."

"And why is that?" Rasheda gathered the abandoned scarves and stuffed them into her bag.

"Because you hug like a straight woman."

Claire's eyes fluttered closed again, and Rasheda studied her face. Amazing to see that pale, knobby skull instead of Claire's wild dark hair. Her emphatic eyebrows had shrunk to thin arched lines, like the penciled brows of a 1940s movie star. Claire's eyelids were veined and tender-looking. Under her eyes sagged thumb-shaped bruises.

This was a woman who had such vitality her very entrance could send energy rippling through a room. This was a woman who once could dance.

Rasheda smiled, remembering the night a couple of years back when she had first discovered this talent. She and Claire were wrapping up a hectic week's work on location in Philadelphia. Rasheda had been relaxing in her hotel room with a mystery novel when Claire knocked on the door and plopped on the other bed.

"It's Saturday night," Claire announced, "and we don't have to get to work until noon tomorrow." She threw her arms wide. "So where would you like to go for our evening's entertainment?"

"Let me think." Rasheda pulled her knees up to her chest. "Someplace lively but not noisy. Someplace where we can hear some music and maybe even dance and not get hit on by men." She sighed. "Someplace that doesn't exist."

Claire bounced off the bed. "Put on your dancing shoes, Ace. We're going to Adelaide's."

The cab dropped them off in front of a stately brick building. Once a private home, now the building housed Adelaide's, a two-story restaurant with a bar and dance floor in the basement.

"Brace yourself, Rasheda," Claire teased. "This is going to be a new experience."

"You think I've never been to a gay bar before?" Rasheda scoffed.

"Yes."

"Okay, you're right." She pulled open the heavy wooden doors. "Let's do it."

They paused at the top of a curving wrought-iron staircase that vibrated with the music. Below them stretched a large, dim dance floor, spattered with reflected light. Beyond that lay a smaller room dotted with round, glass-topped tables. And filling both rooms were women—dancing, talking, laughing, and eyeing the staircase to check out the new arrivals.

"Girlfriend, these women are just cruising you up and down," Rasheda murmured.

Claire turned to her, one eyebrow raised. "What makes you think it's me?"

They did make an arresting sight, Rasheda supposed. Tall, fair-skinned Claire, with her dark, cascading curls, wore black jeans and a black silk blouse pinned at the neck with a silver brooch. Small, round-faced Rasheda contrasted brightly with her baggy blue slacks topped by a gold turtleneck and a kente-cloth vest. The two women skirted the din of the dance floor and settled at a table in the quieter back room.

"This is a busy place," Rasheda observed as they sipped cold beers. "Where are all the men?"

"Are you missing them already?"

"Just curious. The sign said this was a mixed bar."

"It is, but for the most part the men don't get here until later."

"How do you happen to know so much about this place?"

"I used to live a couple of hours from here. Sometimes we'd drive to Adelaide's on the weekends to dance."

"Well, come on, then. Let's see what you can do."

Dancing with Claire was fun and effortless, like dancing with a girl cousin at a family wedding. But there was something else, some kind of edge, that came from Claire's lively black eyes, from the sureness of her touch. Rasheda could see how Claire might be a woman that other women were drawn to.

"You can really work it," Rasheda admitted as they returned to their table. "I was surprised."

"Why?" Claire drained her bottle. "You knew I could dance."

"I knew you could talk about dancing. How was I to know that a white woman could really move?"

"Well, don't spread it around."

"Don't worry. How about another beer?"

Claire grinned. "Think you can fight your way to the bar through all those lascivious lesbians?"

"I'll manage."

"So where do you and Lucy dance?" Rasheda clunked an icy bottle in front of Claire. "There's no place in Sterling that I know of."

"Sure there is." Claire stretched her long legs and laced her fingers behind her head. "You've been there."

"Where?"

"Our living room."

"You two dance in your living room?"

"Sometimes."

"Oh, that's so sweet!"

"Why? Don't you and Kevin ever dance at home?"

"We used to."

"What happened?"

"Keisha."

Claire laughed. "The kid has to sleep sometime."

"If you figure out when, let me know."

"Excuse me," said a polite voice. Rasheda and Claire turned to see a young woman standing beside their table, resplendent in beaded cornrows and a colorful tunic.

"I couldn't help noticing the two of you," she began. "And I wondered if it would be all right for me to ask the sister for a dance."

It took Rasheda a moment to figure out why this girl included both of them in her question: she was inviting Rasheda to dance, and asking Claire for permission. "We're not really together," Rasheda exclaimed. "I mean, we're just friends. What I mean is . . . Look, I'm not gay."

The woman smiled. "It's okay, sister. I'm only asking for a dance."

"Then let's go." Rasheda took the young woman's arm.

She returned several minutes later to find Claire laughing. "That was more than one dance. I think you've got a crush on her."

"Can I help it if they played a few good songs in a row?" Rasheda flopped into her chair. "Hey, I didn't go home with her."

"Well, I am scandalized. You're married, in case you've forgotten."

"So are you, and you danced with me."

"But you're straight!"

"Just because I've already ordered doesn't mean I can't look at the menu."

Watching Claire's sleeping face, Rasheda felt as though that night at Adelaide's had taken place a thousand years ago.

Lucy padded into the living room. "How'd the fashion training go?"

"Not great." Rasheda picked up the doll and the paper bag full of silk. She and Lucy walked to the front door. "But don't worry, I have another idea I think she'll like."

"Good." Lucy leaned against the door jamb. In her faded jeans and white t-shirt, Rasheda thought she looked almost as washed out as Claire. "Are you coming back tomorrow?"

"I can't. I'm working a double shift tomorrow and Tuesday. But if it's okay with you, I'll drop in Wednesday night, after I put Keisha to bed."

"We'll be here." Lucy ran her hands through her fine dark hair. "Rasheda—" she hesitated.

"What is it, baby?"

"I know you're very busy. You're working so much, and Keisha needs a lot of attention . . . The thing is, Claire can enjoy you now. That may not always be the case. I don't want her to go without anything we can give her. And I don't want you to have any regrets."

"I understand."

"I hope you do."

A few nights later, Rasheda sat Claire and Lucy together on the couch. She stood before them and, with a flourish, whipped off a headwrap to reveal her smooth, bald head.

Lucy gasped.

"You cut off the last Afro in America!" squealed Claire. "Why?"

"A gesture of solidarity. Now you and I have the same hairstyle."

"No fair! I look like something out of *Star Trek* and you look like a model."

"You do have a beautiful skull," said Lucy. "What does Kevin think?"

"He thinks it's downright sexy."

"You're lucky," Lucy replied. "And so are we. This is the sweetest thing anyone's ever done for us." She bounced off the couch and gave Rasheda a hug. It was a strong, enfolding embrace. "Two bald girls! I have to get my camera."

∞ ∞ ∞

It occurred to Rasheda now that she had never seen the photo. She would try to remember to ask Lucy about it this evening.

Rasheda stood, stretched, pressed both hands against the giving gray walls of the announce booth. It was time to go home, to help Keisha practice her reading, maybe even to enjoy a few moments alone with her husband.

Across the parking lot, she spotted Gerald in his off-hours uniform of worn khakis and faded polo shirt, the ubiquitous blue baseball cap covering his balding head. "Cooper!" he bellowed as he loped toward her. "It's Saturday! What are you doing here?"

"Just leaving." She unlocked her car door. "What about you?"

"Just arriving. Got a few things to check on, and then—" he pantomimed dribbling a basketball and shooting a basket.

Rasheda smiled at him. He reminded her of Keisha with his fervent enthusiasms. "I'm glad I caught you, Gerald. I wanted to talk to you about something."

"Oh, geez." He sagged against a car. "If it's about that new special-effects generator, I told you we can't afford it."

"It's not about that. It's about Claire."

"Oh." He pulled off his cap and smoothed the fringe of brown hair that circled his skull. "What about her?"

"I just wanted to thank you for keeping her on after . . . after she couldn't work any more. I know the owners were pressuring you to let her go and hire someone else, and I respect you for not giving in. I don't think I ever told you."

Gerald slipped his cap on and tugged the bill over his eyes. "I didn't manage it by myself. Seems to me there was an assistant editor who worked her tail off to make sure we didn't need to hire another hand. I don't know how your old man let you get away with all that OT, with a kid and all."

"Well, he wasn't thrilled. But Claire was my friend. Besides, I'd still be pulling tapes for minimum wage if she hadn't taught me to edit. I owe her."

"Hell, Cooper, you don't owe her squat. Yeah, she trained you, but it was a business decision, and a damned smart one." He grinned. "Fact is, she'd probably say she owed you—for saving her from 'Boys R Us.' That's what she used to call the station before you came along."

Gerald plunged his hands deep in his pockets. "That Claire was somethin' special, wasn't she." With his high-topped sneaker, he traced a line across the black asphalt. "She was a great girl."

"She surely was," said Rasheda, and swung her car door open, imagining how amused Claire would be by the epitaph.

∞ ∞ ∞ **4** ∞ ∞ ∞

A WORLD OF VOICES

"You really need to change it," Jane told Lucy.

"I don't want to."

"I know you don't. But it's time." Noon sunshine looped through the high windows of Lucy's kitchen, turning the light as golden as the scarred oak table where they sipped their iced tea.

"Who says so?" demanded Lucy. "Is there some timetable I don't know about? Am I running late in the grief process?"

"Of course not." Jane kept forgetting how brittle Lucy had become. "All I'm suggesting is, it's too weird to call here and get Claire's voice on the answering machine saying 'We can't come to the phone right now.' It's morbid."

"I know." Lucy gave a tight smile. "But it's just the kind of joke Claire would love."

"Claire's not here," Jane replied gently.

"So I've noticed."

"Well, look." Jane fished a package out of the pocket of her baggy denim shorts. "I got you a tape. If the time comes when you feel like changing the message, you can record a new one on here. That way you can keep Claire's tape and play it whenever you want."

Hands flat on the table, Lucy eyed the package. She rose and walked to the windows, where she stood for several seconds, her face hidden. "Jane, come over here. I want to show you something." Lucy rested her hand on Jane's shoulder and pointed out the window. "Look outside."

"What am I looking at?"

"Just tell me what you see."

Jane inspected the sloping back yard, the ragged lawn, the squares of wildness that had once sprouted rows of vegetables, the tree boughs nodding over the weathered wooden fence like amiable neighbors. "Nothing out of the ordinary," she reported. "Just the usual—grass, trees, plants. A few weeds."

"Okay. Now imagine it in black and white. No, wait. That's not it." Lucy's hand tightened on Jane's shoulder. "Imagine that the view is just the way you see it now, except for one thing. The color green is gone."

"I don't get it."

"Just try to imagine it."

Jane peered through the window, fingers gripping the broad sill. She took off her wire-rimmed glasses and pressed her nose against the cool pane. She stared until tears welled in her burning eyes. Still she could picture nothing but the familiar yard.

Jane started to turn away from the window, and for an instant she saw it. The image was brief and shocking, like the sight of her own face reflected in a falling glass. Dead gray branches poked into a dazzling blue sky. Ashes climbed the back fence and curled around the pink blossoms of the wild rose bush.

Squeezing her eyes shut, Jane tried to recreate the world she had glimpsed. No more welcoming lawns. No fluttering leaves. No trim green shutters on a white cottage. No glistening salads. No busy prairies, no shifting ocean depths. No slow-blinking secrets in a cat's eyes. No more the fresh, giving aroma of new-mown grass, because everything green was gone.

"I think I can imagine it," she murmured.

"That's what life feels like for me without Claire's voice," said Lucy.

"I understand. I miss her too, you know. She's been my best friend since I was 7 years old."

"But you don't understand what it's like for me. It's not the same." Lucy threw herself into a bentwood chair. The front legs reared up and dangled above the checkered floor.

Jane took a long drink of tea. "Probably no one can know what you're going through. But Lucy, you don't help things any. You don't let anyone in."

Lucy folded her arms across her chest.

"It's true." Jane combed her fingers through her wavy blonde hair and pressed on. "When people ask how you're doing, you brush them off. You never give a real answer."

"It's just part of the social contract. People say 'how are you,' you say 'fine.' People say, 'how are you doing,' you say 'better.' They don't really want to know how you feel. They want to know if it's safe to be around you."

"Maybe that's true for most people," Jane argued, "but not your friends. We ask because we really want to know."

Lucy let her chair drop with a thunk. "What do you want me to tell you? That I'm miserable? That I'm in hell? That a hundred times a day I want to say something only Claire will appreciate, make a joke only Claire will understand, ask a question only Claire can answer?" Her voice climbed. "That I can't stand being with anyone who isn't twisted with grief? That I hate all of you because you lost a friend or a colleague, and I lost my *life*?"

Jane tried not to flinch. She knew sorrow shaped people in different ways, and of course she knew better than to ask a grieving person if something was wrong. Yet something seemed wrong between Lucy and herself—something personal. Lucy, who had heaped her harrowing confidences upon Jane, now seemed furious with her.

"Yes," replied Jane in an even tone. "That's exactly what I want you to say."

"I can't do it."

"Sure you can. You just did."

"No, I mean tonight." Lucy drew vertical lines in the condensation on her glass. "I can't have this little anniversary party."

"Oh. I was wondering about that myself. I mean, we all spent so much time together when Claire was sick, and then . . . Well, I haven't even seen Rasheda since the funeral. Have you?"

"Hey, you know who I thought about inviting?"

"Who?"

"Dr. Walker. She's the only one I can think of who went through all of it with us."

Jane swallowed hard. She had hoped she was finished hearing that woman's name. It was never connected to anything but doom.

"We went to see Dr. Walker this afternoon," Lucy had told Jane one summer evening last year. Her voice on the telephone sounded shaky. "All the test results are in."

In the fading light, Jane had stood paralyzed in her living room, clutching the phone with both hands. "What did she say?"

"She said it was unusually aggressive. She used words like 'virulent,' and 'wildfire,' and some words I didn't know. She said that in the best case, Claire will probably die in 6 months."

Jane felt the earth lurch sideways. "And if it's not the best case?"

"It'll take longer."

"Oh, Jesus."

"Jane, I'm so scared," Lucy had whispered. "I'm scared every second."

"It's awful. I can't believe it."

"Claire is the engine of my life. I won't be able to stand it if anything happens to her."

"Lucy, I knew you before you met Claire. You were the engine of your own life."

"That was a long time ago. God, I feel like I'm about to split out of my skin. I'm so terrified I can't breathe. Jane, if I pass out while we're on the phone, will you come right over?"

"I'll come over now. You don't even have to pass out."

"No, Claire is asleep. I just wanted to know you'd come over if I needed you."

"Any time," Jane had said fiercely. "Any place."

And now, a year later, Lucy wanted Constance Walker to celebrate Claire's life with the friends who had loved her? It was the worst idea on earth.

"Then I decided against asking her," Lucy continued. "If I invited Dr. Walker, I wouldn't be able to call this thing off at the last minute. Which I might do."

"Good thinking. Listen, if you can't face it, call me by 6 and I'll tell the others."

Lucy didn't reply, but continued to roll her empty glass between her palms.

With a sigh, Jane pushed away from the table. "I should be taking off." She did have a lot to do this afternoon, and as usual her car was in the shop. It was almost as if the mechanic had gotten custody, and she only got visitation rights.

"Okay," said Lucy. "See you later. Or maybe not."

It was a gorgeous day for a walk. The humidity had lifted its damp veil, leaving the air sparkling and light; the sun gleamed high in the sky like a tossed coin. Jane liked the pace of walking, the human perspective it allowed. Viewing life from behind a windshield felt like watching it on TV.

Now, as she strode past the sturdy houses, Jane could enjoy the details. A man on a porch swing read aloud to his small daughter, unaware she had fallen asleep in his lap. Kids stood on their bike pedals as they zigzagged up the hill. On her knees in the garden, a woman yanked up weeds with a satisfied grunt. A cat rested in the shadow of a large dog.

She should walk everywhere from now on, Jane decided. As soon as she got home, she would call Howard at the garage and tell him to lift her car to the heavens on his hydraulic altar and let it rust there. What a relief it would be! Her universe would shrink to this: the world she could reach on her own two feet, the weight she could carry in her own two arms, the horizon she could see with her own two eyes, the hope she could hold in her own small heart.

Jane remembered how desperate she had been to learn to drive. All her friends had been driving for more than a year, and she could only watch in envy. If it hadn't been for Claire, Jane might never have learned.

She recalled one hazy Sunday afternoon, the summer before they left for college. Claire had borrowed her father's car, a white Chevy Malibu with a black vinyl top, to give Jane a driving lesson. Hurtling down a hill on the outskirts of town, Jane clutched the steering wheel with both fists as the one-lane road coiled in front of them like a snake.

"Speed into the curves," exhorted Claire. "See how a little speed smoothes it out? Keep your foot off the brake!"

Jane didn't respond. She was too busy. Ahead loomed a grocery store.

"Pull in here," Claire instructed. "I want to get a Coke. Then we can practice backing up in the parking lot. You want anything?"

Jane dropped her off and parked in the farthest corner of the lot, under the single shade tree. In an era when to be cool meant a girl had to have long blonde hair, limpid blue eyes, and a football player on her arm, Claire was still definitely cool. All the kids knew it, except Claire. She didn't give a damn what anyone thought. She smoked pot with the heads, played basketball with the jocks, sat on the back porch with Mrs. Van Buren, their English teacher, and argued about the war. On the few mornings when she couldn't cajole the car from her dad, Claire caught a ride to school on the back of Biker Joe's motorcycle. She was way too cool for the bus.

Jane watched Claire saunter across the parking lot, jeans slung low, long arms swinging in her sleeveless denim work shirt. It was weird how different they were, yet how close. Jane had always been skinny, with frizzy blonde hair she pulled back with a rubber band. Her face looked like she had swallowed a light bulb: big cheekbones curving in to a narrow chin. Her pale blue eyes peered out of tortoise shell glasses. Jane avoided groups, hated parties, cringed at loud conversations. She was not cool. And she cared what everyone thought.

Yet they had stayed best friends ever since second grade. Even as high school graduates, they laughed together like children. They made up outrageous stories and dared people to dispute them. They both knew so much about one another that starting over with new friends seemed like work.

Claire plopped into the passenger seat and tossed Jane a small, curvy bottle of Coke. "Driving is all about physics," she explained, planting her sandaled feet on the dashboard. "The faster you go, the more control you have. When you slow down, you lose control."

"But if I wasn't going so fast, I wouldn't need so much control."

"Jane. Do you want me to teach you or not?"

"What do you think? I've got to be the only 18-year-old in Glens Falls who can't drive yet."

"Okay, then you have to do things my way. But I don't understand why your parents don't teach you. They lean on you for everything else. Why don't they want you to be able to run errands?"

"They probably do." The Coke hit the back of her throat with an icy slug. "But my dad doesn't want to teach me because we'd need to look at each other instead of the road."

"Not to mention taking your hands off the wheel to talk."

"Right. And my mom . . . well, you know my mom."

"Yes," Claire had said. "I know your mom."

There were two things Peggy McKay refused to do: drive and sign. Driving was the husband's responsibility, she had often told her daughter, and signing was a concession to weakness. The man had spoken clearly for over 30 years. With a little effort he could do so still. And why should she learn to sign, when he could just as easily—and far more usefully—learn to read lips?

For years, Jane had watched her mother struggle and fail to forgive her husband's slow retreat into deafness. As a child Jane had served as the family communicator, signing messages to her dad, speaking his replies for him. Only now, as Jane herself reached middle age, had she begun to realize what a gift that could be.

"Why don't you come over?" Claire had asked Jane one Saturday morning last summer.

"That's too bad," Jane had replied, phone tucked between chin and shoulder as she watered her plants. "How did you hurt it?"

"What are you talking about?"

"I . . . what did you just say?"

"I invited you to come over. What did you think I said?"

"That you had a bum shoulder."

"You know, this English as a foreign language business is getting old."

Jane watched the water well up and tremble at the rim of the clear plastic saucer underneath her African violet. "Claire, I misunderstood you. It's no big deal."

"You've been misunderstanding a lot lately."

"If you'd use consonants once in a while, it might help."

"Don't try to push this off on me. Have you had your hearing tested lately?"

"Right before we started high school."

"Jane, that was during the Johnson administration! Correct me if I'm wrong, but I seem to recall that your father was deaf as a post."

"Delicately put, as usual, Claire."

"Don't you think you should be more careful about your own hearing?"

"I'm fairly sure what he had wasn't catching."

Claire sighed loudly into the phone. "Look, just come on over. We'll talk about it then."

As she steered her Toyota onto Claire's street, Jane had reminded herself to relax her jaws. Clenching like that was sure to give her a headache. She didn't particularly want to go over to Claire's house right now, yet here she was. Somehow Claire's will always prevailed. Well, this time it would not. Jane would just march right in, visit for a few minutes, and leave. And she would certainly not take any shit about her hearing.

Claire was waiting for her on the porch. "Don't bother getting out of the car. We're going."

Jane threw the car into park and turned off the engine.

"Didn't you hear me?"

"Of course I heard you! I'm not deaf."

"Not yet." Claire snapped her seat belt into place. "What are we waiting for? Let's go."

"I'm not going to a doctor, if that's what you had in mind."

"Relax. We're going to the mall."

Twenty minutes later, they strode down the wide main hallway of the shopping center. "What are we buying?" asked Jane.

"Peace of mind." Claire did not even glance at the beckoning display windows as they passed store after store.

"Where do they sell that?"

"You'll see." At the end of the aisle, Claire steered them left, into a little cul-de-sac. There in the center was a tiny storefront that advertised hearing aids.

"Oh, Claire, for Christ's sake!" Jane turned on her.

"All you do is go in there, take a 5-minute hearing test, and you're done. They don't even charge."

"Why would I do that?"

"Because if they give you a clean bill of health, I'll get off your back."

"These people sell hearing aids for a living. Of course they're going to find something wrong with me."

Claire pulled open the glass door. "Go. I'll wait out here."

"God, you make me so mad sometimes!"

"I know. And I want you to be able to hear every evil word I say."

Jane had stormed into the shop. Fuming, she had sat in the little glass booth, thick padded headphones covering her ears. Through the smoked glass window, she could see the uniformed technician punch some keys to play electronic tones into Jane's ears. With each tone, Jane had raised her index finger—immediately, accurately. No problem. She stood up to leave before the woman on the other side of the window switched on an intercom and announced, "Just one more minute, dear. We have another series to play."

Jane had slumped back into the seat. She waited. She waited some more. What had the woman done, lost the computer program? Jane glanced into the window and met the woman's expectant gaze. Her stomach plummeted as she realized the sounds were already playing, but she could not hear them. Eons passed until she could finally hear something—high-pitched tones that must be attracting every bat from here to Poughkeepsie.

"Are you happy now?" Jane waved a slip of paper in Claire's face as the shop door swished closed behind her. "Look what they gave me. A coupon for $25 off my first hearing aid."

"Does that mean they found a hearing loss?"

"I couldn't hear the damn beeps." Hands in her pockets, Jane studied the fake marbling in the linoleum floor tiles. "Claire, keep this to yourself, okay?"

"Why?"

"Because I want to tell people in my own time."

"All right, if you'll get yourself a real hearing test."

"I plan to."

"When?"

"When I get around to it! You know what's wrong with you, Claire?"

Claire had grinned, her eyebrows quirking upward. "Ooh, I love comments that start like that."

"You always have to go one step too far."

"I do, don't I."

And Claire would have pestered her until Jane was forced to consult a doctor just to shut her up, except that a night or two later, Lucy had found the lump. So it wasn't until this summer—the summer after her death—that Claire had finally gotten her way. Now, as Jane crossed the leafy campus, passing the low brick buildings where both she and Lucy had offices, she steeled herself to learn whether she too was losing her hearing to the same congenital condition that had stricken her father soundless.

The leisurely summer-school ambiance ended at the front door of the university hospital. Over the past few weeks, Jane had spent hours at the Ear Nose and Throat clinic, where the friendly, frenetic staff analyzed her hearing. Under their direction, Jane sat alone in a soundproof room and pushed a button when she heard a beep. She listened to a woman's voice reciting similar-sounding words and tried to repeat them. She allowed technicians to glue electrodes all over her head and time how long it took sound waves to travel to her brain.

This was a teaching hospital, and the clinic was a scramble of interns, doctors, students, and staff. Jane was never sure which doctor she would see, or whether she would ever again encounter a practitioner who had just peered intimately into her ear canal. But as she climbed into the high-backed blue chair in one of the clinic's examining rooms, Jane felt certain she would always remember this silver-haired, gray-eyed beauty who was delicately breaking the news.

"What we have here is a diagnosis, not a prognosis." Dr. Levin perched on the rim of a rolling black stool, her legs braced as if any moment she might need to leap up and send the stool flying. "This condition can result in a range of outcomes, which we don't really know how to predict. In your case, the deterioration is very gradual. You may not suffer significant hearing loss for many years. Or perhaps not ever."

Jane felt her attention split and scatter. Part of her focused on the doctor's words, trying to harvest every drop of hope. Part of her settled into acceptance of the silent future Jane had always recognized as her own. And part of her wandered the room with the gaze of a bored student, noting the way the vinyl seat stuck to her bare legs, admiring the spartan efficiency of the office design.

"If my hearing loss is so minor, why do I have to ask people to repeat themselves all the time?" she asked.

"For one thing, all of us baby boomers are discovering that our nerves aren't quite as conductive as they used to be."

"That's encouraging."

"For another thing, you have particular trouble hearing sounds within a certain range. Unfortunately, the human voice falls within that range."

"Oh, great. So I'll be able to hear garbage trucks and sirens with perfect clarity."

"And bird calls, and many kinds of music, and rain hitting the roof."

Jane considered this. She thought Dr. Levin looked a little like a bird herself, with her feathery silver hair and quick, crisp movements. The doctor's trim body was alert with energy. At the base of her throat beat a calm, strong pulse. Jane wondered what it would feel like to press her mouth against that kiss-sized hollow carved out between the collarbones. Watching Dr. Levin watch her, Jane realized she was pursing her lips. She wiped a hand across her face. "Why did you say I might not ever have any significant loss?"

"Well, we just don't know. It's an unusual condition, almost what we call an 'orphan.'"

"Meaning what?"

"Meaning there's little research done on it, because the condition affects so few people. I know that's not much comfort if you're one of them."

"So there's no treatment."

"Not at this time." She hesitated. "The thing is, Jane, we're not likely to find a treatment unless we stumble on one. To my knowledge, no one is pursuing this particular condition."

"Dr. Levin, you are just full of good cheer."

"I want you to know where you stand. And you're either going to have to start calling me Roxanne or I'll have to start calling you Dr. McKay."

Jane gave her a sharp glance. Was she flirting? The doctor's gaze was direct and sober, but her words left room for speculation. Jane wondered if she would even recognize flirting or know how to respond to it after these 3 solitary years.

"So, Roxanne, is there any good news I should know?"

"Well, let's put this in perspective. You have a fairly rare condition and a measurable hearing loss. But by no means are you certain to experience seriously compromised hearing. Your progression so far is very slow." She glanced at an open folder on the table next to her. "I believe you told me your father was profoundly deaf by the time he was your age."

"When did I tell you that?"

"I was the doctor *du jour* when you first came here to be tested. Oh I know, this place is a medical merry-go-round. It's hard to keep track of all the faces leaning over you. But I was one of them. We spoke briefly before I turned you over to the technicians."

"I can't believe I would forget that."

Roxanne smiled, revealing deep dimples. "I'm devastated myself. But I have an advantage. Some of your students are my patients, and I've heard a little bit about you."

"Like what?"

"Nothing too alarming. Jane, is there anything you're unclear about? Any questions you want to ask?"

"Not right now. I'll probably think of some later, after everything's sunk in."

Roxanne closed the folder. "Then if we've concluded our business, I have a question for you."

"I'm all ears," Jane replied. "Sorry. Bad joke. What's your question?"

Roxanne took a deep breath. "Would you be available . . ." She straightened the lapels of her white jacket. "Would it interest you to go out?"

"You mean with you?"

Roxanne laughed, her face red. "I guess I threw you a curve."

"No, I—it's just that I barely know you."

"I barely know you, too. That's why I thought we might go out together."

"But you're my doctor, or one of them."

"I know. It would mean I couldn't treat you anymore."

"Can you cure me?"

"No."

"Can you slow the progression?"

"No."

"How about Friday night?"

"Wonderful. I'll pick you up. Around 7?"

"Sure. I live at—"

Roxanne held up her hand. "It's in your file."

"What else is in my file? Does it say somewhere, 'likes women'?"

She clicked open her pen. "Do you want me to add that?"

"So how'd you know?"

"The usual way. Gaydar." Roxanne slipped the pen into her pocket next to a tiny silver tuning fork. "Friday night. This is good. My motto is, 'If we're going to be happy, we'd better start right away.'"

Jane peeled herself off the chair. "That's your credo? You may be too healthy for me."

∞ ∞ ∞

Jane dropped the last handful of green beans into the boiling water and watched them dance. The water was playing jazz, but the beans were dancing ballet. At a stately pace, one after another rose to the surface while its partner descended into shimmering shadow. The water jittered and bubbled, occasionally emitting a satisfying hiss when a flying drop spattered onto the stove top.

Reaching for the slotted spoon, Jane wondered if she would miss small sounds like that. Her life was drawing closer to silence, but what kind of silence would it be? The pulsing, solitary silence of swimming underwater? The busy, textured silence of a library? The scared, thumping silence you awaken into late at night?

"What's it like?" she had asked her dad.

"Lonely," he had signed back. "But peaceful. Rich in its own way."

Jane was no stranger to the land of the deaf. She knew its language, its culture, its community. Her life was peopled with friends and students who spoke its eloquent idiom. But now it would be different. Now she would no longer be a visitor.

A pain whistled through her. Normally she would call Claire and tell her about everything: the diagnosis, the date, her hopes, her worries. Now Jane was preparing food for a party to commemorate Claire's death, and there was no one she felt like calling.

She scooped a bean out of the roiling water and took a bite. It was barely cooked, still crunchy, a deep vivid green. Perfect. Dumping the pot into a colander, Jane watched steam rise from the steel sink and disappear against the narrow white ceiling.

No wonder Lucy had refused to remove Claire's greeting from the answering machine, she thought. Now she understood. After all, there was a world of voices Jane would no longer hear. Claire's had only been the first to go.

THE GATHERING

When the doorbell rang, Lucy felt her heart give a little kick. What was there to be nervous about? she asked herself.

If Lucy was not exactly looking forward to tonight, she had at least prepared for it. She had dusted Claire's piano. She had vacuumed the hardwood floors. She had set the table. And she had gotten herself upright, instead of spending the evening as she did so often lately, supine on the couch with her eyes closed, listening to National Public Radio.

Besides, whoever had rung the doorbell and was now waiting with arms full of offerings was no stranger in need of entertainment, but one of her best friends. Lucy tucked her white blouse into her jeans and hurried to the door.

"I'm so glad it's you," she told Rasheda, taking from her a platter wrapped in foil.

"Why?" Rasheda hefted a bulging shopping bag across the threshold. In her pale yellow shorts and oversized white t-shirt, she seemed to bring the summer sun in with her. "Are you expecting some kind of invasion? Is that why you've got this place closed up like a—" Rasheda hesitated.

"—a tomb?" Lucy finished the sentence for her. "No. But for some reason, whenever I see you I get the sense that everything will be all right."

"Well, I'm flattered." Rasheda pulled her into a hug. "So how is everything, baby?"

"All right."

Rasheda paused, as if expecting something more. She released Lucy. "Come on, let's get this food dished up."

As they unloaded Tupperware, Harry strode into the kitchen, followed by Jane. Energetic greetings flew back and forth. Suddenly the quiet house was transformed. Rasheda folded back the wooden shutters and threw open the windows. Jane dropped some jazz on the disk player. Harry seemed intent on rearranging the contents of the freezer. Dazed and pleased by the sudden life in the house, Lucy flitted from one friend to another, handing down serving dishes, ferrying plates to the dining room.

"So that's what you look like when you're not working," Jane exclaimed to Rasheda as they stood at the sink, rinsing fresh fruit. "I knew there had to be a regular weekend person there under all that elegance."

"Yep, nothing glamorous going on tonight," she replied.

"Why not?" demanded Harry. "Don't we rate as much as the guys at that TV station?"

"Harry, I have a young child. I don't have time to be a cutie-on-duty every minute."

"Besides," Lucy interjected, "those clothes aren't really Rasheda. They're just her camouflage."

Rasheda popped a grape into her mouth. "You got it, Lucy. When you're African-American, female, and five-foot-two, you have to project some kind of attitude if you want to deal with the boys in the control room."

Finally they all settled at the round wooden table, festive with its purple cloth and its squat yellow pitcher filled with wildflowers Harry had brought. Breezes brushed the filmy white curtains on either side of the large window; green branches threw dappled shadows against the high white walls of the dining room. The four of them dined on colorful summer salads and crusty bread. They passed around a bottle of light spicy wine.

"I think I'll entertain like this from now on," announced Lucy. "All I provide is the chairs and the tap water, and the guests bring everything else."

Harry helped himself to a huge portion of pasta salad. "A new twist on take-out. I like it."

"Speaking of that, you'll never guess who I ran into last week," said Jane. "Shanti, the woman who's been stalking me."

"How would we guess that?" Harry sounded indignant. "I don't know anyone named Shanti."

"Sure you do. She works at that vegetarian restaurant on Water Street where we used to get take-out food when Claire was sick."

Rasheda reached for the bread plate. "You mean Mary Jane Johnson?"

Jane nodded. "Her name's Shanti now."

"Why is she stalking you?"

"She's not really. It just seems that way because I keep running into her all over town. Last week she invited me to go to some Buddhist thing with her."

"Did you tell her you couldn't go because you're Catholic?" asked Lucy.

"No, I told her I couldn't go because I had aerobics that night."

"I always get those two things confused."

"It's simple." Jane refilled her wine glass. "One requires faith and discipline, and the other doesn't."

"So who brought this wild rice dish?" asked Harry. "It's fantastic."

Rasheda raised her hand. "Yes, I was a cooking sister this afternoon." She turned to Lucy. "And what were you up to today, while we were all laboring in the kitchen?"

"Can't you tell?"

"Um . . . no."

"You don't notice anything different about me?" No one responded. In the brief silence, Lucy reflected on how much she had changed. Grief had carved her up; her very skin looked listless. No wonder her friends did not venture to guess what was different about her. "I got my hair cut."

"It looks very nice," proclaimed Harry, loyally, through a mouthful of crunchy romaine.

"Lucy, your hair only grows an inch every eon," Rasheda pointed out. "You shouldn't let it hurt your feelings if people don't notice."

Jane swept bread crumbs into a pile on the tablecloth. "I too had one of those once-every-eon experiences this afternoon."

"What was it?" Harry's fork stopped halfway to his mouth.

"Someone asked me out on a date."

"Who is she?" demanded Lucy.

"You don't know her."

"How do you know I don't know her?"

"I just know."

"Well, at least tell us her name."

"Roxanne Levin."

"You're right. I don't know her."

Rasheda interceded. "The question is, Jane, how do you know her?"

"I've seen her around. She works on campus." With her knife, Jane shaped the crumbs into a perfect square. Her cheeks flushed a bright pink.

Poor Jane, thought Lucy. With that fair skin and those blue eyes that were so easy to look into, Jane's face published every passing emotion. "Did you say yes?"

Jane nodded. "We're going out next week."

"Why won't you tell us how you met this woman?" pressed Rasheda. "Is it something kinky?"

"No, it's boring."

"Lucy, make her tell us." Rasheda nudged her arm.

"I'm prying my best."

"Jane, let me know if you want any dating tips," offered Harry. "I know you haven't exactly been out there in a while."

"Thank you, Harry. But I think your idea of 'out there' and mine may be somewhat different."

The conversation ambled on to other topics—books, movies, the glut of new coffee shops in town. But Lucy remained attuned to the unspoken topics that hovered above their heads. Jane's peculiar reticence. The absence with which they were all learning to live. And Claire, who drew them all together and who had barely been mentioned throughout the long meal.

It was Harry who finally pushed away from the table and suggested, "Let's move this party out to the porch. We might catch the tail end of the sunset."

"Good idea." Jane began to stack the plates. "This was a pretty remarkable spring for sunsets. I can't remember when they've been so vivid."

"It's the air pollution," Rasheda declared, pointing her wine glass to the open window. "The light refracts through a haze of airborne poisons, and we humans watch it and feel all's right with the world."

Jane snatched the glass out of her hand. "Thank you for sharing, Rasheda."

"Come on," Harry insisted. "We're going to miss it."

Lucy picked up the stacked plates. "You go ahead. I'll be there in a second—I just want to put the coffee on."

So there had been a spring this year, Lucy mused as she spooned the dark grounds. Of course there was, there had to be—New York state's short, startling season of beauty before summer stomped down with its heavy heat. But Lucy hadn't noticed.

She flicked off the lights in the littered dining room. Silently she pushed open the screen door and slipped into a seat on the darkening porch like a latecomer at the theater. Her friends too were silent. Gathered in one corner of the wide wooden porch, they stretched out in the heavy wicker chairs, heads thrown back to watch the sky show. Lucy raised her eyes from the scattered houses in the valley below to the final pangs of pink and lavender stretching above them.

She caught her breath as the night darkened. The stars were endless, clustered so closely they formed streams of incandescent mist. The sky resembled a huge walk-in closet jammed with black sequined evening gowns and diaphanous silver veils. Yet nothing in this tableau was static; the stars shimmied, the planets bobbed. Everywhere above the smooth rising hills the night sky spread its splendor—and all of it, all of it without Claire.

It still astonished Lucy that Claire, who had meant the world to her, meant nothing to the world. She bent her head in surrender to the familiar ache. After a few moments Lucy noticed a strange irregular sound. Looking up, she was shocked to see Harry—eyes squeezed shut, forehead resting in his palm, long fingers threaded through his sandy hair—pounding his fist against his thigh.

She grabbed his bony wrist. "Harry, what are you doing?"

"It helps me sometimes."

"Helps you what?"

"Helps me think about Claire."

She dropped his arm. "Why don't you just let yourself cry? Wouldn't that be easier than beating yourself up?"

"I can't," he replied, eyes still closed. "It's all trapped."

Lucy stared at him. Certainly there could be no doubt that Harry had loved Claire. He loved her with a loud, extravagant love that was almost large enough to hold what happened to her.

When Claire was sick, Harry sent fresh flowers every week. He brought her piles of old movies and later, as she wearied, books on tape. Lucy could call Harry at 3 in the morning, and he would find an all-night pharmacy or a grocery store that stocked what Claire craved. But he could not hold the bowl as she heaved in nausea. With his strong arms, he could not lift her ruined body so Lucy could change the sheets. He couldn't bear it. Perfectly understandable. Who could?

Yet bear it they did: Rasheda with her exhausted eyes, Jane with her deepening silences, Lucy who every day watched the end of her world sidle closer. All of them but Harry. So it was no wonder that Lucy was startled, and moved, and confused to find him speaking his grief with his fists.

"I'm nothing but a feast for mosquitoes out here," Rasheda announced as she rose and beckoned Jane inside with her.

Lucy sat alone in the darkness with Harry. She felt herself suddenly wordless; everything she could think to say sounded false. It didn't matter if he punched himself or cried or tore out his hair. This pain could be eased by only one thing, and it was the one thing neither she nor Harry would ever have again.

"I keep thinking she's got to come back some time." His voice sounded foggy. "I mean, it's like she's playing a big joke on all of us."

"I know. I keep thinking I see her."

"Me too! On the sidewalk, or speeding past in a car."

"A lot of times in the house I'll catch a glimpse of something moving and I'm sure it's Claire, but when I turn my head there's nothing there. Sometimes I think I hear her footsteps."

"You mean like a ghost?"

"No, it's probably just some regular house noise, and I'm used to assuming it's Claire."

"Losing Claire like this . . ." he faltered, "I never imagined a person could feel so miserable. I mean, words like 'bereaved,' or 'mourning,' or even 'sad'— well, I just never knew what they meant before."

You still don't, thought Lucy, and a cold anger prickled her arms in the humid summer night. Your life hasn't changed one iota. You go to your cushy job, you come home to your snug house, you fuck your girls, *what the hell do you know about loss?* She clenched her teeth to keep the words inside.

"I always thought I was strong," Harry continued, "but now I don't know. I don't think I can take much more of this."

"You'll have to," Lucy spat out. "We all will." She swept inside the house, letting the screen door slam behind her.

As soon as she stepped into the bright kitchen, with its soothing sounds of running water and women's laughter, Lucy's shoulders relaxed. "I must be out of my mind," she announced. "I just beat up on Harry for no reason at all."

"What'd he do?" asked Jane, straining to put away a serving bowl on a high shelf.

"Said he missed Claire. For some reason that made me furious. Maybe one of you should go make sure he's okay."

Rasheda turned off the water and leaned against the sink, drying her hands on a dish towel. "Lucy, I take care of men all day and all night. No way am I going to go out there and take care of one that's not even mine. But I'll give you a little advice. Most of the time when you think you've pounded them to a pulp? They don't even notice they've been hit."

"I agree," said Jane, "or at any rate, I defer to the expert. Let's have our dessert in the living room. He'll come in when he's hungry."

Seconds later, Harry wandered into the kitchen, inquiring, "What's for dessert?" He looked baffled but pleased when the three women broke into laughter.

"Look at all this food." Lucy sank into the worn living room couch. They had ice cream, fruit salad, and crunchy thin Italian cookies. They had tea, coffee, and real cream. The feast made a happy mess on the large wooden coffee table. "This is like a second meal. Claire would call this 'take two.'"

"Claire would call this unbridled gluttony," Jane corrected.

Rasheda hoisted herself out of the deep overstuffed chair to put on a Billie Holiday disk. The singer's smoky voice fit the mood of the waning evening. "You know, I don't think any of this food is disgusting enough for Claire."

"That's true," Harry nodded. "She liked really gross stuff."

"Limp, pale French fries dripping with vinegar," Rasheda called out.

Jane responded, "Gooey chocolate chip cookies barely grazed by the oven."

"Runny scrambled eggs sprinkled with jalapeño peppers and green olives," shuddered Lucy. "Ugh."

"So, do you guys think Claire is in heaven?" Harry asked the question in a light, anxious voice that made Lucy suspect he was only half joking.

"Absolutely," Rasheda replied, plopping back into the big gray chair. "I think Claire's in heaven and she's already telling everyone how to do things right."

Jane took up the rhythm. "I think Claire's in heaven and she's ordered new carpeting."

Lucy joined in. "I think Claire's in heaven, and she's got the intake process so smooth the angels only have to work half days."

"That's right," Harry chuckled. "Now, how would she put it? 'Everything's smooth as crystal.'"

"'Easy as cake,'" added Lucy.

"I used to love it when she'd come up with one of those jumbled expressions," Rasheda said. "Which one of you named those 'Clairifications'?"

"It was Jane," Lucy told her. "Just imagine—now there are Clairifications in heaven."

"I think Claire's in heaven," Harry announced, "and she's running for city council."

"You think Claire's wearing herself ragged to run for some city council seat?" scoffed Rasheda. "Child, please. She's already been elected mayor, the mayor of heaven."

Their laughter trailed off into a sad little quiet space. Finally Rasheda broke the silence. "Anyone want to go biking with me tomorrow?"

"Why would we want to go banking with you?" asked Jane.

"Not banking, *biking*. Kevin's taking Keisha on a little father-daughter outing with our church, so it's Mom's afternoon off. How about it?"

"And have my ass fall off at work the next day?" Harry responded. "No thanks. You women wore me out last time." He turned to Lucy. "Remember how Claire kept zipping past me up those hills? Oh, that's right—you didn't go on that ride, did you."

Lucy shook her head. No, she had decided to stay home that day. But she could envision the details as if she had been there: the firm bulge of Claire's calf muscles as she pumped the pedals, her trim butt shifting rhythmically on the bicycle seat, the line of sweat on her white t-shirt branching down her spine and across her shoulders. She could hear Claire's voice describing small animals as they darted into the woods, see her hair fanning out in the breeze.

That bike ride had been one of the countless times over the years when Lucy had chosen to follow her own pursuits rather than do something with Claire. What would she give now to have even one of those opportunities again? Since Claire's death, she had endlessly replayed those scenes, recalling the moment when she could have said yes instead of no, picturing every particular of Claire's face during those lost hours.

And yet—sending Claire off alone to ride the wooded hills, falling asleep with her head in Claire's lap as their rented movie rolled by unwatched, half-listening to Claire's description of her day while Lucy patiently chopped more carrots to replace the ones her partner kept plucking from the salad bowl—these too were acts of love.

"Poor Harry," Jane needled him. "Can't keep up with the girls. What would Cynthia say?"

"She'd say she's not surprised."

"I must have missed an episode or two," said Rasheda. "Who's Cynthia?"

"Harry's latest love."

"Let me guess. Young? Blonde? Blue eyes?"

He grinned. "Gray eyes."

"Glad to see you're embracing diversity."

"Tomorrow night I'm taking her for a moonlight picnic in that meadow up on Stevens Point."

"With the mosquitoes?" Rasheda asked. "And the humidity? And the God-knows-what-all crawls around there at night? Oh baby, if that's dating I'm so glad I'm married."

"It'll be good practice for us. In August, we're going to the beach for a week's vacation. Plenty of stargazing there."

Lucy had been studying Harry throughout this exchange. His lanky body clearly revealed the skeleton he would one day become. Looking up at his face, it would be easy to get a false impression of the man. He had the overlarge square jaw of a comic book hero. His cheeks were flat. You could set a coffee cup on his cheekbones. It was a severe face, with no excess.

But then you got to his eyes, and everything changed. They were deep-set and blue, surrounded by crinkly laugh lines. He was aging like leather, Lucy saw, growing softer with the years. Even now, with dark crescents of sleeplessness shadowing his eyes, he looked comfortable, like something you could sink into.

Lucy felt as if she hadn't seen Harry since Claire got sick, perhaps had never seen him at all. The loneliness of all those hours they had spent together washed over her, and she turned away—just as he swivelled to meet her gaze.

"Rasheda, I'd love to go with you," Jane was explaining, "but I'm visiting my friends John and Miguel in the afternoon. I told them I'd do some yard work for them."

"How's Miguel doing?" Lucy asked.

Jane shook her head. "He's lost about 40 pounds. I'm not sure I'd even recognize him if I saw him on the street. Not that he can walk."

"I just thank God I'm not gay," blurted Harry.

Jane looked up sharply. "Hey!"

"That's not what I meant," he protested, flushing. "Though come to think of it, the thought of having someone's dick inside me does make me want to puke."

"Join the club," muttered Jane.

"It's an acquired pleasure," Rasheda conceded. "So what *did* you mean?"

"Just that I don't think I have the courage to watch all my lovers suffer and die. You know? And be waiting to see which one falls next?"

Lucy turned to him. "Harry," she said, "exactly what do you think is happening here?"

"I know, Lucy, but I'm talking about an epidemic. God knows Claire's death was terrible. But it was just one person."

"That doesn't help if it's *your* one. Besides, you know lots of women who've had breast cancer."

"Who?"

Lucy ticked them off her fingers. "Elizabeth, who used to own the bookstore on Oneida Avenue. Mrs. Chandler at the post office. Melinda, the lifeguard at the pool you belong to."

"My mother died of breast cancer," Rasheda volunteered. "My grandmother, two of my aunts—it's eating up the African-American community."

"Jesus." Harry flopped back in his chair. "I had no idea."

"Well, now you do," Lucy snapped. "Take a good look around, Harry. This is what an epidemic looks like." Her outswept arms encompassed the cluttered living room with its vacant chair, the silent rooms upstairs, and the nearby houses that climbed the dark hillsides toward the unreachable heavens.

∞ ∞ ∞ 6 ∞ ∞ ∞

TV TIME

Rasheda crept into the house, set her empty serving platters on the kitchen table, and locked the back door. From the living room she could hear the nattering of the television. Was Kevin still awake? He could tell her about every adorable thing Keisha had done, and she could tell him all about her night. Then they could cuddle on the couch and talk about how lucky they were.

But when she crossed the dining room and peered into the living room, she saw that Kevin was already asleep in that tidy way of his, feet tucked neatly under the coffee table, hands folded in his lap. He looked for all the world as if he were about to make conversation, except for his large handsome head tipped back against the couch. Nothing would wake Kevin now. Rasheda clicked off the TV and let the swinging door creak shut behind her as she stepped back into the kitchen.

This had been a strange evening, she reflected as she watched blue flame bloom under the tea kettle. First was the weirdness of being in Claire's house without her. That felt a little less strange now, because Rasheda had visited Lucy several times since Claire's passing. But as the months rolled by and nothing in the familiar rooms changed, from the pictures on the wall to the placement of the salt and pepper shakers, Rasheda sensed a kind of hollowness settling in the house, like an early dusk that was just on the verge of becoming visible.

Then there was the strangeness of seeing Jane and Harry again for the first time since everything had happened. Their connection had been so intense during those months while Claire was sick. And yet, before that, Jane and Harry had been just names to Rasheda, heard over a sandwich in the lunch room.

"Jane knows about all the idiotic things I've done, and she doesn't mention them to anyone," Claire had once told her with admiration. "She's got pictures of me dressed up to go *disco dancing,* and she's never even shown them to Lucy. Now, that's loyalty."

Rasheda remembered how surprised she had been when she first met tall, gaunt Harry. He looked nothing like the baby-faced kid brother she had pictured from hearing Claire talk about him.

She pried open a small tin box that held a special Chinese tea Claire had given her. Rasheda had been treating herself to this aromatic tea for a couple of years now, and the box still looked untouched. It was amazing how the tiniest pinch created a whole cup of something so fulfilling. It was like faith, or even friendship. She wondered if friendship was the right name for whatever had been wavering among the four of them tonight.

From the get-go, Kevin had thought her friendship with Claire and Lucy was peculiar. "Office buddies is one thing, but I don't see why you want to hang out with them," he had commented.

"What can I tell you?" she had replied "I'm in with the 'out' crowd."

Rasheda suspected he was uncomfortable, in a fascinated kind of way, with the relationship between the two women. But why was it so hard for him to see that their being different didn't get in the way? In fact, being different was one of the things Claire and Rasheda had in common.

Claire had been convinced that being a lesbian made her a little less white. Rasheda, of course, snorted in derision at this claim. Still, whenever Rasheda would talk about some routine experience—being asked if she knew so-and-so, who happened to be African American, or being expected to represent the views of her entire race whenever she opened her mouth—Claire used to chime in with, "It's the same for lesbians!" It was irritating, even if it was true. But it couldn't be true, because there was no way to tell who was a lesbian, even though Lucy and Claire swore they usually could.

Once Rasheda and Claire had been walking up the sidewalk in downtown Sterling when a woman hurried past and flashed a huge smile at Claire, who grinned in response. "What was that all about?" Rasheda had demanded. "Oh, just the universal 'I know you know' greeting," Claire had explained. Rasheda had scoffed, but darned if a half hour later they hadn't seen that same woman loading packages into a car with a rainbow flag on its bumper.

So maybe lesbians could pick each other out, although for the life of her Rasheda couldn't figure out how. She didn't know what she thought a lesbian should look like, exactly, but certainly not like Claire or Lucy or Jane. She remembered how Lucy had howled when Rasheda had admitted that. They had been sitting across from one another at the kitchen table, sorting Claire's medications into little plastic boxes to organize her dosage for the next few days. "Rasheda, you're in dyke city now," Lucy had declared. "You just don't recognize the landmarks." And Rasheda had been a little embarrassed, but mainly pleased that in the midst of everything she had made Lucy laugh.

But when had Lucy become so solitary? Rasheda asked herself as the steaming water swayed to the top of her mug. She recalled many nights when she used to drive Claire home after work because Lucy had the car and was attending some event on campus, or staying late for a committee meeting, or going out with friends. Where were those friends now? Lucy seemed to cling to only the few who had walked with her through the horror.

Elbows resting on the white wooden table, Rasheda took a sip of the gentle tea. Kevin used to shake his head sadly when she talked about Claire and her friends; he thought their lives were lacking something important. And he was right, but what they were missing wasn't men; it was siblings. Lucy had only one brother, and Claire and Jane had nobody.

Rasheda and Kevin had a whole herd of brothers and sisters, most of whom had kids of their own. All the loving and tussling of a large family made life rich, Rasheda believed—which is why, with more enthusiasm than success, she and her husband had been trying to create a little sibling for Keisha. Although, with her nosy aunts and uncles, and her mess of first cousins, Keisha would probably never have the chance to get lonely.

Clutching her cooling mug, Rasheda crossed the hall to Keisha's room and stood for several seconds in the doorway, watching the 6-year-old sleep with her sturdy arms and legs outstretched, as if even in slumber the girl was running. Rasheda thought of her baby, taking in experience in great gulps and spilling over with sound and energy. It was inconceivable to think that such vitality would one day be stilled. And Kevin, with his powerful arms and loving heart—could she bear to watch him grow feeble, engulfed by suffering?

Rasheda leaned her head against the door frame and composed a silent prayer. "Dear Lord, please keep my family safe. I thank you for your blessings every day." She thought about tonight, about Lucy's strained face and vacant house. Rasheda squeezed her eyes shut. "And please, Jesus," she added, "send that woman some peace."

∞ ∞ ∞

Jane realized she was cheating but she didn't stop. Lots of people knew huge chunks of *The Wizard of Oz* by heart, and she happened to be one of them. So sitting up in bed, watching the old movie with the sound turned off was not helping her reach her goal. It was simply fun, and for tonight that was enough. She would work on her lip-reading skills another time.

She thought she had done pretty well tonight. There had been only an instance or two when she had to ask someone to repeat a comment, just a few occasions when someone's quizzical expression told Jane the question she had answered was not quite the one they had asked. How likely was it, after all, that Rasheda would invite them to go to the bank with her on a Sunday?

It was almost as if Jane had inherited the job of concocting Clairifications. For all she knew, these aural missteps happened no more frequently to her than they did to other people. But by now Jane was so paranoid she couldn't be sure.

Soon she would have to tell her friends, to prepare them for the day when she would be permanently and profoundly deaf. But not yet. For now it was all she could do to chart this strange new terrain of relationships, the landscape of life without Claire. Jane took a sip of lukewarm tea and mouthed, "There's no place like home," along with the silent television.

∞ ∞ ∞

Behind Harry's house a metal satellite dish strained toward the sky like a giant hibiscus blossom. Despite the 150 channels at his command, he could never find anything to watch. At least not after midnight. He lay flat on his back in bed, one hand tucked behind his head, one arm outstretched, wielding the remote control. This was the way he chased sleep every night, and this was the way it eluded him.

He flicked past *Gilligan's Island* and *My Three Sons*. Why were people so fascinated with these reruns? he wondered. Relics of an era when we were all young and stupid? Harry had seen enough of them the first time around.

He flicked past something in Spanish and a show about calculus. There was what's-her-name from *L.A. Law*, looking much better now that she'd dropped that corporate garb. Jill Eikenberry. Hadn't he heard somewhere that she'd had breast cancer? Harry snapped the channel-changer.

Jesus, what was the world coming to? Here was Gloria Steinem, on one of those home shopping channels. He figured she was hawking one of her books, maybe that self-help tome Cynthia kept on her bedroom bookshelf. Suddenly he recalled Cynthia telling him Gloria Steinem had gotten breast cancer too. Or was he imagining that?

How could it be that so many women had breast cancer and he had never noticed? He supposed he knew the bookstore owner had died and the shop had changed hands. And he was vaguely aware that Melinda the lifeguard had been sick a couple of years ago, although she seemed fine now. But Melinda was young and in terrific shape. She was also flatter than Kansas. How was he supposed to guess she had breast cancer?

Lucy had no business jumping down his throat like that. *Why can't you cry?* she had demanded. Like he could help it. Like any of this was his fault. She was the one who hadn't noticed the lump until it was too late. Well, he would cut Lucy some slack, but he would never understand her.

Harry was channel-changing furiously when he thought he heard a dash of Claire's voice, or a similar one. Low, confident, sounding like it could break into a laugh at any second. He backed it up. No, not that show. Not that one either. There. Jane Fonda, playing a TV reporter hot on the trail of some cowboy.

Harry scooted lower in the bed, pulled the sheet up to his chin, closed his eyes. She didn't sound all that much like Claire, but it was relaxing listening to her; he felt himself smiling in the dark. He should go to the video store and rent a bunch of her movies. Although come to think of it, Jane Fonda hadn't been in many movies lately.

Harry's eyes flew open. He hoped to God she wasn't sick.

∞ ∞ ∞

At night, wandering the acreage of an empty bed, Lucy taught herself to live in TV time.

"A minute is an eternity in television," she remembered Claire saying. It had been ages ago, the first time Claire had shown Lucy around an editing suite and tried to interpret its mysteries for her. "The unit of time I use is a frame, which is a thirtieth of a second. Each edit I make has to be accurate down to the frame."

"That sounds pretty demanding," Lucy had replied, and continued her fascinated examination of the sterile room, kept chilled for the comfort of machines, with its constant twilight and bewildering banks of monitors, keyboards, levers, and buttons lit up in rows of color. So this was the place in which Claire happily surrendered hours of her life, breaking seconds into tiny fragments.

"How in the world did you decide to be a TV editor?" Lucy had asked over lunch that day. "As far as I can see, every one of your colleagues is a fat white man addicted to donuts and Diet Pepsi."

"That's not true!" protested Claire. "Some of them are skinny white men addicted to coffee and cigarettes."

"So where do you fit in? What are you addicted to?"

"I'm addicted to you, baby," Claire replied in her best tough tone.

"Of course you are. But what were you addicted to before you met me?"

Claire smiled over her sandwich. "I was addicted to the mystery. Editors harness this very exacting technical process, yet what the viewer experiences is information and emotion. It's like a mixture of science and magic—turning electrons into art."

Later Lucy would wonder if there was something about those electrons, something about that busy room and its emanations of cold light that had caused a cell in Claire's body to run amok. But she asked those same questions about everything—the house they lived in, the car they drove, the food they ate. Wondering what had happened was what Lucy did at night while she learned to live in TV time, where hours were elastic, minutes were eternal, and seconds split into slow-moving particles that sometimes drifted into dreams.

Tonight Lucy dreamed Claire was walking toward her. Claire's thick dark hair was tied back with a black ribbon; she was wearing jeans and a flowing white linen blouse. She was smiling. They were outside, among a milling crowd of people. Music was playing; perhaps it was some kind of summer festival. No one else seemed to notice that Claire had come back from the dead.

The two women approached each other slowly, with a deep calm happiness. As Lucy reached up to kiss her, Claire slipped a white gauzy handkerchief between their lips with a look both flirtatious and sad. Lucy realized they were not to touch.

"I'm thinking of all the ways I won't be able to love you," Lucy murmured as they stood inches apart.

"Think of all the ways you've loved me already," Claire replied.

The faraway band started a new song. Claire pulled on white cotton gloves so they could dance without touching each other's skin. But as they swayed, the white linen blouse pulled up ever so slightly, and Lucy's hand on Claire's waist found warm flesh.

Suddenly they were at home, in their own bed, making love. Lucy could hear Claire's urgent murmurs, could feel the taut, muscular trembling of her thighs. In the dream they came together, their bodies clasped, their cries mingling in the heated air.

Lucy awoke into sunlight, weeping in gratitude for the joy Claire could give her, one last time.

∞ ∞ ∞ **7** ∞ ∞ ∞

FULL CIRCLE

Jane set her grocery bags on the cushiony grass while she opened the mailbox. She never knew what her hand would meet in that dark recess: a package, a bank statement, a spider. Today it was junk mail and her copy of *Rolling Stone*.

Jane was pretty sure she was the only 45-year-old on earth who still subscribed to *Rolling Stone*. It was embarrassing, yet it was important to her in some strange way. She rarely listened to the music the magazine discussed; the bands she had loved were mentioned only occasionally, gathering for a reunion, or making a cameo appearance in some tongue-in-cheek movie.

Jane's students also did not listen to music in any typical fashion. But they stamped their feet at concerts, flung themselves wild at dance parties, wore t-shirts emblazoned with the names of bands. So Jane read *Rolling Stone*. It was a way to enter her students' world and enliven her own.

As she unfolded the magazine, a letter slid out. Thin and light, it seemed to hang in the air before wafting to the pebbled driveway. The envelope was made of crinkly, light blue Air Mail paper, the corner crowded with colorful stamps.

Jane glanced at her mailbox, hanging open like a gaping jaw, and thought it was mimicking her own expression. The letter must be from Coralie.

In more than 3 years, she had not heard a word from Coralie. One day the woman had simply vanished. Jane had received only one message, a postcard with a picture of JFK airport. On the back was scrawled "It was hot. Thanx." There was no signature, but none was needed. The card sported the same bold, left-leaning hand as the letter Jane now held.

Theirs had been a hot blaze, all right—fierce and swift. It had burned cleanly through Jane, leaving nothing behind, not even a scar. Oh, she had been upset when Coralie disappeared, of course; baffled, angry, hurt. But not devastated. All those dramatic emotions of her youth seemed to vanish with her thirties.

Since then, Jane had gone out briefly with a few women, but nothing took root. Now it seemed she could barely remember passion, any more than in February she could recall the sting of sunburn. Which made Jane wonder why she had just spent 45 minutes at the grocery store stocking up on supplies that might come in handy tonight if Roxanne wanted a drink before they took off on their first-date adventure.

Jane plunked the bags on the butcher block counter of her narrow kitchen and began to unload. A good bottle of chardonnay in case Roxanne was a connoisseur. Three flavors of seltzer water in case she was a nondrinker. A jug of spring water in case she was a purist. A liter of ginger ale in case she was just like Jane and wanted her refreshments to sparkle and tingle as well as quench.

She unpacked a chunk of caraway-studded Havarti cheese, two boxes of crackers, a roll of tiny rye bread. She pulled out bags of carrots and celery, a plastic tub of Greek olives, a carton of nonfat yogurt. It occurred to her that she had bought enough snacks to throw a party but nothing to actually cook for the next week.

What would Claire think if she could see Jane now? Jane could picture her, leaning against the door jamb, thumbs hooked in her belt loops, shaking her head. "Getting a crush on your doctor," she would say. "What a cliché." Smiling, Jane stuffed the groceries in the refrigerator and hurried into the living room to open the sky blue mystery that had winged its way across the ocean.

Anyone could tell in an instant that Jane lived alone. The hip-shaped indentation in the burgundy cushion of her favorite chair was a dead giveaway. So was the single excellent reading lamp, which curved over the back of the chair as if trying to read over her shoulder.

Jane loved her house. True, it had the look of belonging to someone who had spent too much time in graduate school: mismatched furniture, a profusion of books crammed into assorted bookcases, creamy walls decorated with framed posters interspersed with sketches and watercolors done by artist friends. Still, it was cozy, and it was hers. She had paid off the mortgage with money she inherited when her father died. It had taken every penny of her inheritance plus all her savings, and Harry had advised against it. But Jane couldn't be budged. The legacy she valued from her father had nothing to do with money. And now she had a tenured job and a paid-off home—two huge items she could cross off the worry list of adult life.

Jane plopped into her chair, propped her sneakers on the oval glass coffee table, and pulled Coralie's letter out of the back pocket of her jeans.

'Dear Jane,' she read. 'I hope this finds you well and happy. Basically, I hope this finds you! I can't picture you anywhere but that funky little house, so I guess you must still be there. Sorry about the way we parted. It was rude, I know, but things were crazy then and so was I.' Jane snorted.

'I just wanted to let you know I landed on my feet. After a lot of wandering and crazy adventures, I found myself in Israel. Now I am married and the mother of a son. He's 9 months old. I remember the kinds of things I used to say about men, but Ariel (my husband) is different. A gentle soldier. And I will raise my son to be a good partner to some woman who maybe is not even born yet. I know all this must sound weird to you.'

"Oh, just a tad," Jane muttered. Coralie had hated children, despised all things military, scorned any activity that could be considered remotely domestic. She wasn't even Jewish. And she was a dyke! Or at least she used to be. Now she had reconstituted herself into a new person bearing no resemblance to the old. Why had she bothered to write to Jane?

'I guess life goes full circle,' Jane read. 'Write me if it feels right. *Shalom*, Coralie.'

"Write if it feels right. Puh-lease." Jane crumpled the letter and tossed the weightless ball from hand to hand. The funny thing was, it did feel right—not to become pen pals with Coralie, but to learn how things had turned out for her. Jane could not imagine Coralie in the life she had described, but the woman seemed content. Good for her. And good for Jane, too, to finally unscrew the cap to that particular jar and let the butterfly go free.

She pitched the balled-up letter to the ceiling and snatched it out of the air with one hand. It reminded her of the crinkly, smeary typing paper she had gone through by the ream when she was writing her dissertation. What ever happened to typing paper, she wondered. Was it stuck in some office supplies museum, next to carbon paper and Korrectype and those hard thin eraser disks with the stiff brush tails? And why was she musing about the demise of the typewriter when she had only 2 hours to tidy her house and prepare for Roxanne?

Something—Coralie's letter, Roxanne's approach, the leisurely decline of this beautiful summer afternoon—was making Jane feel positively jolly. Slouched in her favorite chair, playing catch with herself, she smiled. It was an amazing thing. Claire was dead, Jane herself was going deaf, and here she was, feeling jolly. Life goes full circle.

∞ ∞ ∞

Despite all Jane's preparations, Roxanne did not want to stop in for a drink. Instead she put her little red Jeep in gear and whisked Jane to a secret destination.

"A bowling alley?" Jane exclaimed as they pulled into the parking lot.

"Yes! It's the perfect place for a first date. We can have dinner in the little yuppie diner and spend the evening getting to know each other while wearing really ugly shoes."

Jane stared at Roxanne but couldn't see her eyes behind her dark glasses. "How many first dates have you had here?"

"See?" Roxanne yanked up the emergency brake. "That's exactly the kind of question we can ask each other while they reset our pins."

The diner, of course, was called Strikes 'n' Spares. Jane and Roxanne took a seat in a booth near the back. Each table was equipped with salt and pepper shakers shaped like bowling pins, and a tiny personal jukebox that glowed like an altar between the ketchup bottle and the chrome napkin holder. Jane wondered if people really played the jukeboxes, or if the distant slam and thunder of bowling balls was music enough.

They gave their orders to a young waitress wearing a turquoise dress cinched at the waist by a white apron. A dapper white handkerchief peeked out of her breast pocket, matched by the little white cap perched on her startling auburn hair. Her crooked plastic name badge read "Maude"—in quotation marks. Except for the six gold rings in each ear, the woman was a pretty good throwback to the 1950s, an era her parents probably remembered only dimly.

"Okay, it's truth time," Roxanne smiled at Jane as the waitress strode away in her squeaky white shoes. "Brace yourself."

"Oh no," groaned Jane. "Are you going to grill me?"

"We'll start with something easy," Roxanne promised, but then she posed a baffling question.

"What did you say?" demanded Jane.

"I asked how long you've lived here. What did you think I said?"

"'How long is your red hair.' I know it makes no sense, but that's what it sounded like to me."

Roxanne tilted her head. "So you have to process what you hear to decode the meaning."

"Sometimes. I have to sift the sounds through screens of logic to figure out what the person is most likely to be saying. That's why it takes me a while to respond sometimes. People probably think I'm slow-witted, but I'm just running the options through my brain."

"I wish more people would stop and think before they speak. So how long *is* your red hair?"

Jane chuckled. "About 10 years. I moved to Sterling after doing the usual academic shuffle from school to school."

"What made you choose this university?"

"They offered me a job. They have a good program here, so I grabbed it."

"How is it a hearing person was hired to run the program? I thought the deaf community was pretty determined that deaf people should fill those roles."

"And some school administrators are equally determined to have a hearing person do it. It's easier for them. In my case they felt they were splitting the difference, since I grew up signing. But of course I still have an accent."

"An accent?"

"A hearing accent. Native users of ASL can tell in an instant that I learned it as a second language."

"Just by the way you move your hands?"

"Sure."

"I never knew that. Some of my patients must be pretty amused by the way I sign."

"I think they cut us hearing folk a lot of slack."

"Where did you grow up, Jane?"

"A little town upstate called Glens Falls. This region feels like home to me. How about you?"

"I grew up in St. Louis. Moved here about 3 years ago, seeking serenity and wisdom. But they eluded me." Roxanne wore black jeans, a red linen blouse, and a black silk vest dotted with a red paisley design. Silver glinted on her fingers, her wrist, her ears. On her feet were beautifully tooled cowboy boots of charcoal gray. In contrast to her delicate appearance, the butch vest and boots functioned like a big fat wink.

Jane too had dressed carefully for this outing, in khaki slacks and her favorite forest green blouse, rich in hue and silky with age. In the summer Jane longed for light colors, but with her fair complexion, wearing pastels made her feel as if she had disappeared. No matter how much time she spent outdoors, a spray of freckles

across her nose and cheekbones was the only concession her skin made to the seasons.

"Sounds like a tough way to begin life in a new
town," said Jane.

Roxanne shrugged. "I landed in a pretty good
place. Engrossing job, gorgeous area, and all the snow
a girl could want."

"Don't they have snow in St. Louis?"

"City snow. This is different."

"Are you a skier?"

"No, I just like to play. Mainly I like to walk in the
woods when everything is white and silent. And I love
to sculpt snow creatures on my front lawn."

"That must make you popular with the neighborhood kids."

"Yes, they like to dismember them."

'Maude' returned with their dinners—a huge
Greek salad for Roxanne and grilled chicken for Jane.
Normally Jane would cut all her chicken into bite-sized
pieces right away so she would never again have to look
up from her book. Since she was on a date, she re-
frained.

Roxanne removed the anchovies from her salad
with surgical precision. "So what do you do when
you're not charming your doctors?"

"I like to read, take walks, cook. I love movies."

"So do I!" cried Roxanne, as if that was an extraordinary coincidence.

"Sometimes I have little gatherings for my students." She laughed. "I always find a few of them
huddled together in some corner of the house, studying
everything as if they've stumbled onto the artifacts of
some extinct culture."

Roxanne speared a chunk of cucumber. "I'm not a
big believer in that."

"You don't think you can learn about a person by examining the possessions they choose to live with?"

"Well, how much of your furniture did you choose? A lot of mine is castoffs from my friends."

"Good point. That must be why you would barely step over the transom this evening when I invited you in."

Roxanne's eyebrows shot up. "Oh, did you want me to stick around? I thought you were just being polite. Maybe you'll invite me in again tonight, when I take you home."

Jane's heart gave a little flip.

"What about adult friends?" Roxanne asked. "Don't you hang out with anyone who remembers, say, the Mickey Mouse Club?"

"Sure. I have a whole gang of faculty friends, and of course regular non-work friends too." She frowned. "Actually, it's kind of complicated right now. My best friend died a few months ago."

"Oh, I'm sorry."

Jane nodded. "And now things are a little weird with her partner, Lucy, who's also an old friend of mine."

"Weird in what way?"

"I'm not sure. Things are shifting with this group of us who were close to Claire and helped take care of her when she was sick."

"What do you mean, shifting?"

Jane was silent for a few seconds, thinking. "Have you ever watched a flock of birds sitting on a telephone wire? When one bird flies away, the others all rise up, and there's a lot of flapping and fluttering before they settle back down."

"Maybe it's a question of balance."

"Maybe. Anyway, we all had dinner together last week." Jane pushed a spear of broccoli around her plate. "I didn't tell them."

"Tell them what?"

"That I'm about to lose my hearing."

Roxanne set her fork down with a clatter. "Jane, you're not losing your hearing. I certainly hope I didn't give you that impression."

"Not exactly."

"You have a condition that sometimes can lead to deafness. There's no indication it will happen to you."

"What about my dad?"

"Your progress is already vastly different from his. There could be any number of factors that affect it." She reached across the table and touched Jane's hand. "Please don't assume you're going to follow the same path as your father. There's no medical reason to believe that." She smiled, displaying her dimples. "Besides, I'd have to hang it up right now if I thought we were all doomed to follow in our parents' footsteps."

"Why? Don't you like your parents?"

"I adore my mother. If I could be more like her I'd be thrilled. My fear is I'll turn out to be like my father. Not that I exactly know how he turned out."

"What happened with him?" Jane could still feel Roxanne's touch on her skin, even though both of Roxanne's hands were on her own side of the table, fiddling with the silverware.

"Oh, you know, the old story. Left us when I was 9 and my kid sisters were 7 and 5. Rarely came to see us. Sent checks sporadically. Then he got remarried and dropped us entirely. Bought his new family a house in the suburbs, while my mother supported all of us in public housing on a nurse's salary."

"Have you ever seen your father since you've be-come an adult?"

"Why would I want to do that?"

"Because you seem so angry at him. Maybe now you could tell him that."

"Maybe so." Roxanne made a physical effort to change the mood. Jane could see her shoulders shifting under the silk vest. "Hey, what kind of first-date talk is this? We're supposed to be finding out whether any of your exes have ever been involved with any of mine." She signaled to 'Maude,' and they ordered coffee.

"So what makes this a date?" mused Jane as she stirred milk into her mug.

"What do you mean? Were you uncertain about my intentions?"

"Not for a minute. It was clear from the way you asked me."

Roxanne adopted a French accent. "Was it ze way I gazed deep into your eyes?"

"No. It was the way you stammered."

"I thought I was pretty smooth."

"You were bold, but you weren't smooth. Anyway, this is more of a philosophical question. What makes tonight different from any time two dykes decide to have dinner together and bowl a few frames?"

"Ah, the classic lesbian date dilemma. I think the defining factor is not the activity, but the context."

Jane gestured at their surroundings. "You mean a romantic ambiance? Subtle lighting? Soft music?"

"No, none of that. Any activity, anywhere, be-comes a date if it takes place in the proper context."

"And what would that be?"

"A context of erotic possibility." Roxanne tilted her head. "And I believe tonight qualifies. Would you agree with my assessment, Professor?"

"Why, yes," said Jane. "I would."

∞ ∞ ∞

It turned out that Roxanne was a terrible bowler. With tremendous concentration, she could knock down a handful of pins. Her most emphatic body language could not make the ball more responsive—it merely made her performance more comical.

Jane, who barely scored higher than her age, felt like a champ in comparison. She laughed until her stomach hurt. "What in the world made you choose to go bowling tonight when you're so bad at it?" she asked as they climbed into the Jeep.

"I thought it would be fun. I have this rule: I try to laugh seven times a day. Next week at work will be pretty grueling, so I figured it might be a good idea to get in some extra laughs this weekend."

"Stockpiling your fun. That's such a cold war concept."

"Isn't it though?"

Jane listened to the automotive symphony: the hum of the tires, the growl of the engine when Roxanne shifted gears, the squeaking seats, the jingle of the keys as they knocked against Roxanne's knee. Strange that all of these distinctive sounds could mix together and recede into something like silence. "Does it work, this laughing rule?"

"It works for me. I'm a pretty happy person. Do you have any rules?"

Jane thought about 'speed into the curves,' but it seemed too complicated to explain. She glanced at Roxanne in the underwater light of the dashboard. "One rule is, you have to come in when you take me home."

"Do you have anything to drink? Bowling is thirsty work."

"I'll find something."

A half hour later, Roxanne planted herself in Jane's hallway, studying the framed photographs that lined the wall.

"I thought you didn't believe in getting to know people through their home furnishings," Jane pointed out.

"Pictures are different."

Jane stood behind her and squinted over her shoulder at the familiar photos, trying to see what they could be telling Roxanne. Claire leaned against an old stone wall, a water bottle dangling from her outstretched arm. Lucy looked up from a book, laughing. Jane's mother plunged a spade into her vegetable garden. Decked out with a fishing rod and vest, her father gave a goofy grin and displayed his empty catch basket. Half a dozen colleagues from Jane's Ph.D. program clowned for the camera, flashing the sign for "cheese."

She had thought Roxanne was so petite, but at this proximity it was clear there was only an inch difference between their heights. Jane took a step closer. She felt as fizzy as the ginger ale she had poured for Roxanne.

"Jane," said Roxanne without looking at her. "Either you need to stand back or I need to sit down. My legs are getting all wobbly."

"Which should it be?"

"Oh, let them wobble." Roxanne wheeled, grasped Jane by the upper arms, and kissed her.

Jane felt a searing joy sweep through her. She was alive. She was alive, and for this one clanging moment she was not alone.

It was an ordinary thing to kiss a woman—ordinary yet utterly miraculous. Jane remembered it now. Crushed against Roxanne, a wildness rising in her skin, Jane remembered it all. She remembered passion. She remembered wonder. She remembered the sweet, sharp magic of the things we take for granted.

∞ ∞ ∞ **8** ∞ ∞ ∞

EXILE

In all the times Lucy had reached for this polished wooden door, never before had she faltered. Tonight her fingers froze an inch from the handle, and she stood there dumbly, waiting for her hand to make up its mind.

"We could go somewhere else," pointed out Amy. She looked not at Lucy but at the sidewalk, where a papery green leaf scuttled away as if startled by her words.

"No," said Lucy. "This is our favorite restaurant."

"It doesn't have to be." Amy's partner Sarah took a step backward, down the sway-backed wooden stairs. "We could find a new one."

Lucy yanked open the door. Her stubbornness was instantly rewarded, as the familiar aroma of garlic, cinnamon, and fresh-ground coffee embraced her. You could walk in here blind-folded, thought Lucy, and still know you were in Mrs. Peel's.

The three women settled into one of the cozy, over-decorated grottoes of the reclaimed Victorian house. A waiter rushed over, crying "Ladies, welcome back! We thought you'd abandoned us." Bryan looked unchanged, Lucy noted, with his elegant dancer's body, his glossy short hair, his gorgeous hazel eyes.

"Bryan, how've you been?" asked Sarah.

He handed each of them a heavy, padded menu. "Busy, busy, busy." Cradling the last menu, he hesitated. "Will the other lady be joining you?"

"Not tonight," Amy replied, and flipped open her menu before Lucy could catch her eye.

It settled around Lucy then like a heavy cloak, the unnameable feeling she had come to know so well. So many times she had tried to throw off the sensation, so many times she wished she could simply dash herself against something dark and harsh and ugly instead of dragging through the days carrying this weight of longing that would surely stretch her bones. Lucy was surprised her arms and ankles didn't jut out of her clothing, surprised she didn't go lurching through life like a Giacometti figure. Mostly she was surprised that no one else could see how utterly alien the world had become. "Why did you do that?" she asked Amy.

"Do what?" As assistant manager of street services for the town of Sterling, Amy spent many winter nights in the glare of snowplow headlights, shouting instructions into a walkie-talkie as snow pelted her orange jumpsuit. All that authority evaporated as she peered at Lucy, her blue eyes guileless above the menu.

"Why did you tell Bryan that Claire wasn't joining us tonight?"

"Well, she's not, is she?"

"She's not joining us any other night, either."

Amy curled a lock of light brown hair around her finger. "I know, but I figured you wouldn't want to get into it."

"What is there to get into?" pressed Lucy. "We say 'She's dead,' he says 'I'm sorry,' and that's all there is to it."

"Lucy, I think Amy and I may have both misjudged the situation," interjected Sarah. She was tall and imposing, with striking russet curls and eyes to match.

Sarah was a massage therapist—a body worker, she called herself, which always made Lucy picture her friend pounding dents out of fenders. Winter or summer, Sarah dressed in long, roomy skirts and scoop-necked blouses the color of jewels. Dangling from her ears were silver swirls symbolizing the four winds.

Claire used to say Sarah "danced to the tune of a different drummer." In fact, Sarah did move with the sound of bells, gold and copper bangles sliding down her muscled arms. It irritated Lucy now that Sarah seemed to be using her professional voice—calm, soothing, and a touch condescending. "I didn't realize Bryan was so important to you, Lucy."

"It's not for Bryan, it's for me." Lucy looked at her friends across the busy flowered tablecloth, across the centerpiece of dried pods and pine cones, across the gulf that separated her from their bright, puzzled faces. "Don't you see? I want Claire's death to be acknowledged. When you pretend it never happened, it's like you're erasing her, and me too."

Amy touched her fingers to her lips. "I'm sorry, Lucy, I never meant to erase you. This is all new to me. I guess I don't really know how to act."

"I know. It's new to me too. I just—I keep trying to tell people what it feels like."

Sarah smoothed the napkin across her knees. "Help me understand, Lucy. If you're not trying to go on as if nothing has happened, why did you want to come to this restaurant, where the four of us always used to go? Why not find a new spot that could be our place"—she gestured to the three of them—"instead of *our* place?" Sarah's long arms encompassed the familiar square table and its empty chair.

"Because I like Mrs. Peel's, and so do you. Besides, if I tried to cut out everything I associate with Claire, every place we used to go together . . . well, I'd be exiled from my own life."

Bryan appeared at their table, bearing a basket of Mrs. Peel's famous dinner rolls. Flourishing silver tongs, he bestowed on each plate two steaming rolls, whorled as rosebuds. "Would you ladies like anything to drink?"

"God, yes," blurted Amy. "A glass of chardonnay for me, please. And Bryan, this lady"—she gripped the arm of the vacant chair—"this lady won't be having anything. She's gone."

"Gone?"

"She passed away. She died."

"Oh! I'm so sorry." Bryan turned to Lucy, and his beautiful eyes filled with tears. "When did it happen?"

"In December. Right after Christmas."

"Well, I'm glad to see you back here. It's not easy, but it's all part of the battle plan."

"What do you mean?"

"Death is greedy. He'll snatch your life too if you let him. You have to fight for it inch by inch, like a lost homeland. But I see you know that already." With his thumb, Bryan twisted a silver ring on his right hand. "I lost someone too, you know. Seven years ago."

"What was his name?" asked Lucy.

"Daniel." He savored the word. "His name was Daniel."

"Bryan, why don't you bring a glass for yourself when you come back and we'll drink a toast to Daniel and Claire."

"Oh no." He smiled. "Louise would have my head if she caught me drinking with the customers. Besides, tonight is for the living. Drink a toast to your friends here."

"Yeah," Amy echoed. "Drink a toast to us." A few minutes later they did—Amy with her wine, Lucy with her decaf, Sarah with her sparkling water and lime.

"It feels like a hundred years since we've gotten together." Lucy broke open a roll. "What's been going on in your lives? Tell me everything."

"Well, it's August," began Amy, chasing a cherry tomato around her salad plate. "That means my life at work begins to narrow down to the essentials: salt, sand, and steel."

"I understand about the sand and salt, but what's the steel?"

"Snowplows. I'm obsessed with them. I even dream about them—snowplows and spare parts. The end of summer is an anxious time down at the roads department." She speared the tomato. "Gotcha!"

Lucy turned to Sarah. "And do you share this infatuation with snow removal equipment?"

"Hardly. But I have my own little infatuation going on these days."

"What's that?"

"This intensive course on acupressure I've been taking at the Holistic."

"The Holistic?" repeated Lucy.

"The Holistic Health Center, down on Watervliet. You know, behind the Honda dealership." Sarah picked up a wedge of lime and munched the fruit without even a pucker. "It's fascinating, learning about all the points and the energy pathways. I'm thrilled about it; I think it'll add a whole new dimension to my work."

"You should let her practice on you, Lucy." In her white silk blouse and taupe linen blazer, with her toffee-colored hair pulled back in a French braid, Amy looked serene and elegant. Lucy wondered if she should have dressed up a little for this evening, instead of pulling on her black jeans and a maroon cotton shell. "It really feels great," Amy continued. "When Sarah's finished you can practically feel the energy zinging through you. Of course, Sarah does have the best hands in the business." The two of them giggled; this was apparently an old joke.

Lucy closed her eyes against sharp memories of the mornings when, raising a coffee cup or bending over her notes, she would catch the faint fragrance of Claire on her fingers. Whose signature could she wear on her skin now? Only her own. And she was dry as dust.

Blinking at the rose-rimmed bread plate, empty but for a few golden flakes, Lucy saw her future. "Yes," she said. "If you're looking for people to practice on, I'll volunteer."

"I'm so glad," exclaimed Sarah. "I need the practice hours, and I really do think it will be good for your spirit."

Bryan swiftly cleared the table and presented their main dishes. Sarah sliced into her medallions of free-range chicken, decorated with crisp green peapods and disks of carrots. "So what are you doing for your spirit these days?" she asked Lucy.

"You mean, like church?" Lucy took a melting bite of fish, the three flat strips drizzled with trails of tangy lemon-caper sauce.

"No, I mean what are you doing to help yourself feel better?"

"Oh. Well, until now I've been pretty much holed up in the house. There's a lot to do when someone dies. Practical decisions to be made, all kinds of legal and financial materials to organize, endless paperwork—I was surprised. And after that, I just wanted to retreat from the world for a while."

"What about school?" asked Amy.

"You know I took last semester off, and I'm taking this semester off too. I can't imagine having the energy to teach. Ultimately I may decide to do something else for a living. But I think work is not really what I need right now."

"Have you joined a bereavement group?" Sarah balanced a peapod on her fork.

"I haven't really thought about it. But if I did join a group, I don't think I'd tell anyone."

"Why? It's no cause for shame."

"I know, but I wouldn't want to raise anyone's expectations that I'd keep on attending. I'd probably just want to drop in. A commitment is the last thing I need."

"What do you need?" Amy twirled pasta around her fork. Black clam shells ringed her flat white plate like shields.

"Stillness, I think."

Sarah nodded. "That's good. You know, I wish Claire had found more stillness in her life."

"Sarah, don't," warned her partner.

"No, I'm going to say it. Amy doesn't agree with me, but I often worried about the level of stress Claire had to deal with."

"What do you mean? Claire didn't have that much stress."

"All those high-priced, split-second decisions at work? All those deadlines? And, well, you two were always running late. But when you're alone, you're perfectly punctual. So it must have been Claire who couldn't break away, or couldn't get organized, or whatever it was. And that's a lot of stress right there."

Lucy snapped her mouth shut. Certainly there had been plenty of occasions when she had paced by the front door, jangling her keys, while Claire called out from the bedroom, "Hang your horses, Lucy! I'll be right there." But it wasn't the way Sarah described, not at all.

"You don't understand. Claire was late a lot, but it wasn't because she was busy tearing her hair out with anxiety. It was because she enjoyed what she was doing so much she hated to stop and go on to the next thing. I mean she hated to get up in the morning, and then she hated to stop drinking coffee and reading the paper, and then she hated to quit work at the end of the day. And that's how it went until she hated to go to bed at night."

"That's a lot of hate," Sarah pointed out.

"Sarah, you don't know what you're talking about. You're going to base a life analysis on the fact that we kept you waiting a few times?"

"Look, Lucy, I've noticed it in my practice and I've noticed it among my friends. People who invite stress into their lives tend to get sick more often."

Lucy slammed down her fork, making Amy jump. "Don't even start that, Sarah. I'm not going to sit here and listen to you suggest that Claire 'invited' cancer into her life."

Sarah exchanged a glance with Amy. "All I'm saying is—"

Lucy cut her off. "I don't care what you're saying. You don't get a vote. Where were you while Claire was sick? Yeah, I know, you dropped off a few casseroles. But you weren't *there*. So don't you dare try to judge how she lived her life, or how she died."

Sarah stared at the tablecloth. "I'm sorry, Lucy. I always respected the way Claire made her decisions. I would never judge her."

"But you are judging. What would you call it, when you claim she got sick because she didn't manage her stress properly? You don't have any dim idea how Claire got cancer. No one does."

"Even the doctors don't know much about it, do they?" Amy ventured. "I mean, they don't know what causes breast cancer or how to cure it."

"They're the worst! I remember one of the first specialists Claire talked to, Dr. Thompson. He gave us this little sermon about risk factors. Well, none of Claire's close relatives had breast cancer, she didn't smoke, she exercised regularly, she ate red meat maybe a couple of times a year. So where's the risk in that?

"Then he started intoning something about 'lifestyle factors,' as if Claire had chosen her disease along with her wardrobe. Well, I was ready to deck him because I thought he meant being a lesbian. But no, that wasn't it either. He meant that Claire had never had children. He made it sound accusatory. Needless to say, that was our last consultation with Dr. Thompson.

"Then we found Dr. Walker, and she just threw up her hands at any talk about risk factors. 'Claire is female,' she said. 'That's the only risk factor that counts.' Turns out most of the women who get breast cancer don't have any of the known risk factors."

"But maybe there are other factors," Amy said slowly. "And maybe they are lifestyle choices, but not necessarily the kinds of decisions individuals can make." She pushed her plate away. "I mean, I have to make choices all the time about the chemicals we use to patch the roads or kill the weeds in the median strip. A lot of times the most cost-effective solutions are the most poisonous ones, and I have to fight like hell to avoid using them. I don't always win, either."

Marshalling her leftover capers into a straight line, Lucy thought of the chlorine that whitened their laundry, bleached the paper they wrote on, disinfected the pool where Claire swam her diligent laps. She thought of the chemicals that each summer turned Sterling into a chain of verdant parks and lawns, of the low-flying planes dropping their dawn spray on the fog of mosquitoes that lifted off the lakes. Perhaps all the things that made life in these wooded hillsides comfortable and convenient and affordable would, in the end, make life impossible. How much could one life hope to be worth, after all, in the bone-chilling bargain of the market-place?

"What did we used to talk about," Lucy wondered aloud, "before Claire got sick?"

"Oh, you know," Amy replied. "Work, movies, books, politics. Other people. The mainstays of lesbian discourse."

"Oh yes, let's gossip," exclaimed Lucy, but it was no use. Grief had made her too self-centered to muster any lasting interest in the vicissitudes of other people's lives.

"It doesn't feel right between us, does it," observed Sarah. With both hands, she pushed her heavy auburn hair away from her face. Bangles chimed down her arms. "Maybe it will take some practice for us to get our balance back."

"I guess I'm not ready to socialize like a normal person. I know it's been almost a year, but time moves so strangely for me now. Each day takes forever to get through, but the weeks and months seem to evaporate."

Sarah patted her hand. "We all grieve our losses in our own time."

Lucy signaled for the check. "Whatever that means."

∞ ∞ ∞

Later that evening, Lucy had just finished washing some stray dishes when the telephone issued a muffled summons. She peered into the dusky living room for the handset.

As long as she could remember, the cordless phone had resided next to its base in the kitchen. Now that she

106

was alone, Lucy could never find it. All those years Claire must have rescued the phone from wherever Lucy had abandoned it. So smooth had been their symmetry that Lucy was surprised to discover her own careless habits. Where was that ringing coming from? She glimpsed white plastic peeking out from under a couch cushion, and lunged for it.

"Hello, Lucy? This is Estelle Benjamin."

Lucy paused. The name was familiar, and so was the high, pleasant voice, but she couldn't quite place them. "Yes?"

"Perhaps you don't remember me, dear. We met at Claire's—at the funeral. Estelle and Morris Benjamin, from Duluth?"

"Oh! Aunt Stella and Uncle Mo." Suddenly the image leaped into place: not of Aunt Stella, but of Claire's animated face whenever she mentioned her favorite relative. "I'm sorry. Claire told me a lot about you, but I don't think she ever used your full name."

"No, I suppose she wouldn't."

In the brief silence, Lucy observed herself in the wavy mirror of the black, unshuttered windows. The living room was dark, and in the distant glow from the kitchen her moving figure cut a shadowy silhouette, a traveling blankness.

Estelle continued, "You know, dear, Claire spoke of you so often, and so lovingly, that I felt compelled to call and see how you were getting on."

"That's very kind of you. I'm doing a little better now, thanks."

"Lucy, did Claire ever tell you that I lost my husband?"

She caught her breath. "Uncle Mo?"

"No, no, my first husband. Claire was only a baby; she probably didn't even remember him. But I do. I remember what it felt like when I was rounding the corner toward the first anniversary of his death. It was the worst time of my life—worse even than the night of the accident. That's why I wanted to call you, Lucy, to see how you really are."

Lucy let herself sink to the floor in front of the couch. She felt safe there, her legs pressed against the broad wooden planks from which she could fall no farther. "Oh, Aunt Stella, I'm so miserable."

"Tell me, honey."

"I can't."

"Why not?"

"It's hard to talk about. And the truth is I can't quite picture you. I met so many of Claire's relatives that week, at the service and sitting shiva at her parents' house. I was in such a daze myself, I barely remember any of it. To me you're mainly a character in Claire's stories."

"Well, what's wrong with that?"

"But which one are you? Describe yourself."

"Oh, let's see now. I have gray hair, blue eyes. I don't wear glasses. I'm a bit rounder and quite a bit shorter than Claire's mother."

"What were you wearing at the funeral?"

"A teal suit."

"No, I'm sorry. I can't place you."

"Lucy, what does that matter? We know all we need to know: Claire was special to me, and you were special to Claire. Her voice used to get all twinkly when she talked about you."

"It did?"

"Certainly."

Lucy closed her eyes. "Do you remember how she laughed in that funny way, with no sound except little squeaks?"

"When she was a child, she had an adorable little giggle. I suppose that was gone by the time you met her."

"Not entirely."

"Tell me about your life with Claire."

"Like what?"

"Oh, I don't know. An anecdote. Some kind of story. Tell me about your first fight."

"Our first fight." Lucy leaned her head against the sofa. "Let's see. I don't think we argued much at all the first couple of years. The first time I remember fighting, we had just moved into this house. Claire was being bossy about something, but I can't recall what it was. Oh, I remember! It was about our back fence."

"That's a new one. Do tell."

"Well, we have this nice old wooden fence that surrounds our backyard. But it ended just beyond the kitchen door. So when you were in the kitchen, looking out the screen door, all you could see was this little wooden enclosure. Claire hated that. It made her feel like our back door opened into a jail yard. She wanted to pull down the gate and lengthen the fence."

"And you disagreed?" asked Estelle.

"No, I thought it was a good idea. But I wanted to do it later, after we finished the inside of the house. Claire insisted it had to be done now. It was the silliest thing, but for some reason that fence brought out the stubbornness in both of us."

They had been sitting on the bed, Lucy recalled, the deep blue bedspread stretched like a sea between them. Claire had grabbed her sweatshirt from a drawer and flounced into the bathroom, where the falling sun threw her shadow against the half-closed door. Lucy had watched the shadow yank the sweatshirt over her head, punch her arms into the sleeves, toss back her hair. She remembered finding even Claire's shadow beautiful. Then Claire closed the door with a click, and it was over: the smooth, unrippled sweetness of never having quarreled was gone forever.

"What happened then?" Aunt Stella's voice seemed no more vivid than the click of the bathroom door.

"We started digging up fence posts. And you know what? Claire was right. Changing that fence opened up the vista and brought in the light. It took us months to paint and strip. And each morning, when I opened the kitchen door to the sun, I was glad we had started with the fence."

"So your first fight was about the back fence?" Estelle asked. "You don't find that peculiar?"

"I guess it is kind of symbolic," Lucy agreed. "Talk about your boundary issues."

"No, I meant it's so—impersonal. It's like having a lover's spat about the prime rate."

"Oh, no, it was completely personal. The argument wasn't about fence posts, it was about how things would get done in our household."

"And how did things get done?"

"Mostly by negotiation. Sometimes by stealth." Lucy chuckled. "I remember one year Claire decided to surprise me by installing these shelves I had wanted above the clothes rod in our bedroom closet. It was all very sneaky; she took the day off and did it while I was at work."

"And were you surprised?"

"Absolutely. And so was Claire, when she realized I could barely reach them. Of course, she had based it on her own height. So she was mostly the one who used the shelves. I'm still not sure what's up there." Through the front windows, Lucy watched the porch furniture flare and surge in the fleeting beam of headlights. "I suppose I'll have to go through that stuff soon."

"No you don't. Not a moment before you're ready."

"When your husband died—what was his name?"

"George."

"When George died, did you ever dream about him?"

"Terrible nightmares, about what his last moments must have been like. Then, for a long time, nothing. It wasn't until much later that I began to have sweet dreams. They were like delightful visits, but so rare."

"I hardly ever dream about Claire. I wish I could."

"I know."

Lucy tried to imagine Estelle. Was she too sitting alone in an unlighted room? As they talked, did Estelle sew, pace, pet a drowsy cat? Lucy couldn't envision the scene, and she was glad. Aunt Stella was only a voice in the dark, a sound of pure comfort.

"The thing is . . ." Lucy began.

"What, dear?"

"The thing is, I'm afraid I'll forget what she looked like. Before the cancer, I mean. I remember everything about that. Little bits of horror keep floating up to the surface. I'll be at the gas station filling up the car, and suddenly I'll see her writhing in nausea on the couch. But Claire herself, when she was healthy, her lively, open, laughing face—that's what I don't want to forget."

"What I found was, don't look at too many photographs at first. Those static images can stick in your mind and crowd out your own living memories."

"Claire never wanted us to get a video camera. She said it was too much like her job. Now I wish we had videotaped it, all of it."

"You did, dear, in your mind."

From her seat on the floor, Lucy wondered if that would be enough. How could she ever retain it all,

Claire's melting dark eyes, the softness of her skin, the pale freckles on the back of her neck? Would she even remember tonight, this moment, with her living room etched in moonlight and the melody of a stranger's voice on the line?

"Now you tell me a story," said Lucy. "Tell me something about Claire, something you think I might not know."

"Where to begin?" Estelle fussed comfortably. "I always thought Claire was an extraordinary child. Of course, all children are extraordinary, but she had a kind of gleam that you could tell would last into adulthood."

"Gleam. That's a good word for her." Lucy heard a rustling sound, as if Estelle were settling into some cushioned nook.

"I can see her now, with her little black eyes bright as buttons, and that big poufy cloud of curls. She was engaging, and talkative, and so inquisitive. Everything interested her, even adult things most kids don't notice. How did the milkman know how much to bring? Why did Mrs. Cameron next door always look so sad? Oh, and here's a funny thing. Claire loved absolutely strange foods. Her favorite treat as a child was a mayonnaise and olive sandwich on rye bread. I do hope she grew out of that phase?"

"Not far," replied Lucy. "She was disgustingly fond of sardines on graham crackers. 'It's the juxtaposition of salty and sweet,' she would tell me. 'You know, like chocolate-covered pretzels.' As if one abomination could justify another."

"So many children are timid about food, but Claire would try anything. And not only food. I understand that in high school she drove her poor parents mad, experimenting with drugs and such. But by then Morris and I had moved to Duluth, so I missed that era."

"I forget—are you related to Claire's mother or father?"

Estelle laughed. "Why Lucy, I'm not related at all. We were friends with the Morgansterns, lived on the same block. In those days there weren't many Jewish families in Glens Falls. We pretty much lived in each other's kitchens."

"Claire always described you as a relative."

"I'm flattered. Yes, Claire and I stayed close, even after she grew up. Especially then."

"When did she first tell you she was a lesbian?"

"She didn't have to. She came to visit me the summer after she graduated from college, and she brought a girl. It was perfectly evident from the way they looked at one another that they were in love. She was a darling girl. Let's see, what was her name? Libby? Beth?"

"Betsy."

"That's right, Betsy. And later there was another girl, and another, and probably a few more. And then there was you."

"So what did you think of it, this parade of girls?"

Estelle hesitated for only a moment. "I worried about the hardships Claire would face. You know, few things in this world evoke more hatred than the crime of love. And I thought how terribly sad for Muriel and Frank to have no grandchildren. But in a way I was not surprised. I had often imagined Claire's path would be adventurous, although to be honest, that particular direction never occurred to me. Still, Claire always seemed too full of zest to live a conventional life."

"That's kind of funny, because the life we lived was very conventional. I mean, we went to work, came home, cooked dinner, washed the dishes. There was only one thing different about the way we lived."

"But that one thing was a whopper."

"I suppose. Still . . ."

"What is it, dear?"

"I wonder if secretly she longed for a bigger life than the one we shared."

"What do you mean, bigger?"

"Well, there were so many things Claire was interested in, so many things she never got to do. She wanted to speak Spanish, go kayaking in Alaska, play the cello. She wanted to learn to *embroider*, of all things. I wonder, in the end, if she felt cheated." They had never been to Europe, thought Lucy, never seen the Grand Canyon. What had they done with all their years? "You know, Claire's work friends say her skills were too advanced for this market. She could have worked anywhere, New York or Los Angeles. But Claire had a partner who was tenured at the local university. So she stayed here."

"Lucy, don't even think such a thing! Claire never felt that you held her back. Besides, she would have been miserable living in a big city. Naturally you have regrets. We all do. But try to remember things as they really were."

Lucy rose and walked to the windows. "How do I do it, Estelle? That gleam, that zest, everything that was Claire—how do I keep it all alive now that Claire is gone?"

Lucy heard a sigh. In the scratchy telephone silence, she had time to watch a lone bicyclist labor up the hill, his headlamp carving a wobbly yellow cone through the darkness.

Finally Estelle responded. "I don't know the answer to that, Lucy. But I can tell you one thing: talk about her. Bring up her name. Quote her. Speculate about what she'd think of this or that. After a while your friends won't mention Claire. They'll be afraid to remind you—as if you could forget. Or maybe they're afraid to remind themselves. All I know is, don't give in to that type of silence."

"Is that what happened to you?"

"I let it happen. Of course, George died more than 40 years ago; naturally the memories have blurred. But I feel like I've lost so many details. Did he have a birthmark? Laugh lines? Ugly feet? What was his favorite book, what funny expressions did he use? I can't remember. I let him go too easily, Lucy, and for the most feeble reason: to keep other people comfortable."

"I won't do that, Aunt Stella."

"No, dear, I'm sure you won't. Claire always said you were the strong one in the family."

After they hung up, Lucy lifted her corduroy jacket off the coat hook and slipped out the back door. It was a strange night, chilly but humid. The weathered boards of the fence felt damp as she pressed her palms against them. Feeling her way down the fence line, her face so close she could smell the musty planks, Lucy slowly paced the length of the back yard.

Could Claire really have thought Lucy was the strong one? If so, she'd be pretty disappointed right about now. Lucy didn't feel strong; she didn't feel much of anything, except a heavy, sodden misery. She was far from dead, but hardly what you'd call alive.

Claire, on the other hand, just kept getting deader. With each canceled subscription, each page torn off the kitchen calendar, each revolution of the earth, she vanished a little more.

The day would come, thought Lucy as she inched her way along the fence, when every moment would not be crowded by Claire's absence. The day would come when the people Lucy encountered would be simply themselves, instead of not-Claire. The day would come when Lucy would sleep in the middle of the bed, take up the whole closet with her clothes, choose any chair at the kitchen table. And on that day Claire would truly be gone.

Lucy wheeled and flopped against the fence, her head thrown back to the sky. She gasped; her hand crept up to her mouth. Spanned across the blackness was the eerie, elegant sight of a rainbow cast by the moon. Pearly arcs in varying shades of silver, from pale to charcoal gray, shimmered in the darkness. It was the loveliest thing she had ever seen, and the loneliest—all the colors of night arrayed like a sad smile across the face of the August sky.

∞ ∞ ∞ 9 ∞ ∞ ∞

THE VACATION

On the third day of his vacation, Harry awoke to the sight of Cynthia leaning over him, smiling, as sunlight gilded her blonde hair. It was morning. He had slept through the night for the first time in months. He could not believe how wonderful everything looked—vivid, colorful, wiped clean of the smear of exhaustion through which he had viewed the world for so long.

He grabbed Cynthia and covered her face with noisy kisses that made her giggle. "I have a great idea, Cyn. Let's take a walk on the beach. We can have breakfast in that little restaurant on the pier."

"That's over a mile away," she protested.

"You can work up an appetite. And if not, maybe they'll let you order from the children's menu. You never eat enough for an adult-sized meal."

"That's one of the things you love about me." She pushed him down on the bed. "You get to eat all my leftovers."

"Come on. I'll carry you piggyback if you get tired."

Harry did carry Cynthia part of the way home, running ostrich-like while she clutched his sunburned shoulders and squealed until he dumped her into the soft sand in front of their bungalow.

All day long he felt giddy with well-being. His energy was endless; his cheeks hurt from smiling. If this was what one night's sleep could accomplish, imagine what life would be like if he slept every night.

"I think it's because I wore you out," Cynthia boasted later that afternoon as she dribbled sand down the length of his lanky body. Harry was stretched out on his back after a strenuous game of Frisbee. She was kneeling over him, apparently trying to bury him in slow motion. "I'll bet if we had great sex every night and played on the beach every day, you'd get over your insomnia in a hurry. I'd keep you too busy to think those dark thoughts."

Eyes closed against the sun, Harry smiled. "And as soon as you win the lottery, we can do that."

"Where would we go in the winter?" She smoothed a pile of sand across his chest.

"Hmm, that's a tough one. St. Croix? Cozumel? The Riviera? Where do the rich and famous hang out these days?"

"We'd have to do some research. But would you really let me keep you if I were rich?"

"Sure thing. I'd be your houseboy."

"Good. Let's start practicing right now." Cynthia brushed the sand from her hands in a ticklish shower over his stomach. "I could use a nap, houseboy."

"But I'm not tired." Harry squinted up at her. He didn't want to lose any part of this wonderful day.

"Not *that* kind of a nap."

"Oh, I get it. A love nap," he crooned.

"Bingo."

"Great idea. I'll race you to the house."

Harry was rubbing his face between her small breasts, his long fingers cupped around them, when he felt it. It was like a seed, or a piece of gravel. A raisin.

He leapt off the bed. "Oh shit!"

Cynthia bolted upright and clutched the sheet to her throat. "What? What is it?"

"Jesus, Cyn, you've got it. I felt it. You've got a—you know, a—a—" He thought he would vomit if he had to say the word 'lump.'

"On my left breast? Oh yeah, I know about that. It's okay, hon, it's just a cyst. I get them all the time." She reached out her arms to him but he took a step backward. "Harry, come back to bed. You look like you're fixing to faint."

"We gotta go. We gotta go right now."

"Harry, you're acting crazy. Look, give me your hand. It's okay, just give me your hand." Cynthia held it to her left breast, gently pressing his index finger. "Right there? Is that what you felt?"

He nodded.

"Honey, it's a cyst. I've had at least half a dozen, and they've all felt just like this. When we get back next week, I'll make an appointment with my doctor. She'll take care of it right there in her office. It's no big deal."

Harry sat heavily on the bed. "Just to be safe, I think we should get it looked at right away."

"Where? On this island?"

"No, at home, with your doctor. If we left now," he glanced at his naked wrist, then grabbed his watch from the bedside table, "damn, I guess we still couldn't make it in time. We'll have to go to the emergency room at the Sterling hospital."

Cynthia gave an incredulous laugh. "Harry, I don't even have insurance. I'm not going to an emergency room for something I know is a routine office job."

"I'll pay for it."

"No way. I'll see my regular doctor, not some intern."

"Okay, then let's call and make an appointment for tomorrow. We can leave first thing in the morning."

"There's no phone here."

"We'll drive into town and find a pay phone."

"I don't want to leave. It's only Tuesday. You rented this house for a week."

She was staring at him with such an astounded expression that Harry realized how ridiculous he must look, hopping around in a panic with his shrunken little dick bobbing. He slipped on a pair of boxer shorts.

"Cynthia, I know we've prepaid. I don't care about the money."

"Well, I do," she retorted.

"Look, I paid for the house. I'll pay for another one later, after we've gotten you checked out. Please, just let me get you back to Sterling. Your health is more important to me than any vacation. Please, babe."

Cynthia stalked to the chair to pick up her shorts and t-shirt. Harry stared. He had never seen her move like that, without a trace of self-consciousness or seduction. It was very beautiful but at the same time it made him shiver. When she yanked the shirt over her head, her gray eyes were a stony color that was new to him.

"Listen, sweetie. I'm real sorry about your friend that died. But I don't have cancer. I have a cyst." Cynthia slapped the pillow against the headboard and plopped down cross-legged, facing him. "Now, I've been saving up for this trip—not just money, vacation days too. I only get 10 each year, and no one can pay those back to me if I blow them in a doctor's waiting room."

Harry took both of her hands in his own, massaging her palms with his thumbs. "But Cynthia, think for a second. What if it is cancer?"

Coolly she withdrew her hands. "Then I'll still have it next week, when I get back. Harry, I know what's best for my own body. Now, I'm staying, and

I'm having myself a vacation. If you can't deal with that, maybe you should go on home."

For a full minute, Harry stared at the sandy wooden floor. He imagined spending the rest of the week with Cynthia in the little house, anxiety clawing at him. No matter what they did, where they went, what she wore, he would know the lump was there, growing. No way could he touch it again. Without a word he stood and began to pack.

Probably Cynthia was right, he reflected as he drove miserably homeward through the slanting shadows. Probably it was a cyst, just like the ones she had had in the past and might have in the future.

But Harry told himself he would not know about Cynthia's future, because on that afternoon he had renounced love. Never again would he rest in a woman's embrace. Never again would he caress a woman's breast and feel the death within her. Women were too fragile for him, and too doomed.

$\infty \infty \infty$ 10 $\infty \infty \infty$

THE GARDEN CREATURE

"I love being middle-aged," Lucy had exulted on the morning of her forty-second birthday.

"That's my girl, born to be mild." Claire handed her a mug of coffee and slipped into bed beside her.

"It's so freeing. I feel much more sure about myself than I used to, much less concerned about other people's opinions. Plus I have everything I want in life." She leaned her head on Claire's shoulder.

"Then I guess you won't be wanting the birthday gifts I got you."

"Wrong."

"But how could anyone who's so stuck in the mud want anything new?"

"Not stuck," Lucy had corrected. "Just settled in."

Claire used to sleep on her side, with one arm flung over Lucy's waist. Each night Claire rested her head on a pillow so thin it resembled an envelope bearing a long, intimate letter.

Now Lucy clutched that pillow to her chest as she lay on her back, staring at the white dimpled ceiling. Today was her forty-fourth birthday, and she could not think of a single reason to get out of bed.

She felt like a garden creature, inching through her middle years leaving a shiny, gruesome trail of firsts. The first time she set the table for one. The first time she spoke about Claire in the past tense. The first time she woke up alone on her birthday.

Nothing had prepared her for this. The books, the articles—they don't tell you what it's going to be like, thought Lucy. Or maybe they do, but it's truer than they can make you believe. But then, what use were warnings? She remembered a summer afternoon last year, when Claire's doctors were still trying to map her disease.

"Lucy, stop jiggling your knee like that," Claire had snapped as they sat hunched on orange vinyl chairs in the ominously cheerful waiting room of the radiology department. "You're making me nervous. Why don't you take a walk?"

"I want to be here."

"I know, but they're just going to take some pictures. These folks can shake'n'bake my boob without you watching."

"I don't have to go in with you, if you don't want. I'll just wait out here."

"The thing is, I'd like to be alone for a minute before they call me."

"Oh. Okay." Lucy rose, but she couldn't make herself leave. Claire looked so vulnerable in her brave new jeans and the hospital's flimsy tissue tunic, her wild dark hair tamed by an elastic band. "I'll, um, maybe I'll go call Jane."

"Good idea."

Lucy tried to walk off her anxiety down the sharp-smelling hallways of the hospital. Her sneakers made erratic squeaks on the shiny linoleum. Fluorescent lights throbbed. Rounding a corner, she was startled to see a colleague scuffing toward her in paper slippers and a billowing hospital gown.

"Sally! What are you doing here?"

"I just had a baby. Eight pounds, three ounces. A little girl."

"Oh, well, congratulations. What's her name?"

"Never mind that now. Listen to me." She clutched Lucy's arm. "Nobody warned me. It hurts like hell. Don't let anyone tell you it doesn't. I thought I'd split in two. My husband was useless. He took videos." Sally's fingers dug into Lucy's skin. "Promise me you'll remind me if I ever talk about having another child. Promise me!"

"I promise."

Sally wheeled and tottered back down the hall.

Lucy recalled a passage from *The Bell Jar* in which Sylvia Plath described a drug she said only a man would invent, a drug that allowed women to experience all the pain of childbirth but then erased the memory of it. Bending to slurp from one of the hospital's strangely unrefreshing water fountains, Lucy resolved that when life got back to normal she would find the quote and share it with Sally.

But normal life was over. Later that afternoon a hoarse-voiced radiologist tapped his ballpoint pen against a backlit row of mammograms and illuminated the future. In silence Lucy had studied the images: Claire's breast a dark planet, the tumor an exploding star. Doom.

Lucy rolled onto her stomach and pulled Claire's pillow over her head. Would her life always be like this, a net of memories, one thread leading to another, with Lucy trapped inside?

The phone shrilled once, twice. Lucy considered letting the answering machine get it, but then she would have to listen to her own carefully upbeat greeting. She lurched out of bed and lunged for the receiver.

"Hey, birthday girl. You still up for a visit?"

"Oh God, Rasheda." Lucy glanced at herself in the bedroom mirror. "I'm sorry, I forgot all about it. What time is it?"

"Almost ten. Did I wake you?"

"No. I'm just a little out of it."

"Well, do you still want us to come over?"

"Us?"

"Keisha and me. I could swear we talked about this last week. Does this conversation ring a bell with you?"

"Yes, come on over. That would be nice. But give me a few minutes to get ready."

"How about half an hour? We're walking. Keisha wants to collect some autumn leaves."

∞ ∞ ∞

"Look what we found!" Keisha unzipped her red, strawberry-shaped backpack and dumped a pile of leaves on the living room floor.

"Nice, Keisha," laughed her mother. She tossed her leather jacket over a chair and gave Lucy a hug. "I guess this isn't one of your happier birthdays."

"No." Rasheda's skin felt smooth and cold against her cheek. "It's kind of funny," said Lucy. "I feel like someone has pushed the 'pause' button on my life, but the years keep unreeling anyway." She looked into Rasheda's round face. "Do you ever feel like that?"

"Can't say I do." Rasheda glanced down at her daughter, engrossed in sorting leaves into piles. "Nothing like a kid to make you feel your life's stuck on fast forward."

"Next year I'll be Claire's age," Lucy mused. "After that I'll be older than she ever got to be."

"Aunt Lucy, come look!" Keisha demanded. Lucy squatted beside her on the floor.

"Here's a red leaf, and here's a gold one, and here's an orange one. And this one's all brown and crinkly." Keisha crumbled it between her hands. "And look. This used to be a leaf, but now it's a skeleton." She touched it reverently with a stubby forefinger.

Lucy wanted to scoop Keisha up in her arms. She was so precious, with her sturdy little body, her brown shining puppy eyes. How could Rasheda bear it, knowing she could never protect her daughter? Nothing but luck stood between one heartbeat and the next.

"What's this?" Lucy asked, pointing to a piece of the treasure.

"Stick." Keisha swept it to the side. "But lookit, here's a twig with a dead bug stuck to it. The bug must have died eating this twig."

"Yum."

"Lucy Rogers!" admonished Rasheda from the kitchen.

"What?"

"Am I looking in the wrong place, or are you really out of coffee?"

"Oh, yeah. I was planning to go to the store today."

"And what are you doing with this nasty milk, trying to make cottage cheese?"

"That's right."

Rasheda bustled back into the living room. "Baby, aren't you eating?"

"Of course I am."

"Give me your car keys."

"What for?"

"I'm going to run to the store and pick up a few things."

Lucy crossed her arms. "Rasheda, I don't need any caretaking."

"You are all the way wrong about that, child. But who said anything about taking care of you? I'm wasting away here. And you know Claire would kick both our butts if she found out there was not a single bagel in this house on a Saturday morning."

"That's true."

"Keisha honey, do you want to come to the store with me or stay with Aunt Lucy?"

Keisha didn't bother to look up. "Stay here."

"Okay." Rasheda grabbed her jacket. "Lucy, when she's done playing, be sure to have Keisha sweep up that mess. She knows how."

After a few enraptured moments, Keisha lost interest in her nature study. As she took the whisk broom from Keisha, Lucy tried to imagine managing a first-grade class bubbling with such evanescent enthusiasms. Undergraduates seemed difficult enough to engage. "Would you like some hot cocoa?" she asked.

"Yeah! With marshmallows?"

"I don't think so. It's the instant kind that comes in a packet."

"Plain is okay. I'll be right back." Keisha raced up the stairs.

As the kettle began to hiss, Lucy climbed on a chair to rummage through the top shelf of the cupboard. She was not sure what she would find up there; high shelves had been Claire's domain, along with changing light bulbs and cleaning above the refrigerator. She pulled out the box of cocoa and noted that the expiration date was still 2 years away. Apparently the stuff lasted forever.

Keisha settled at the kitchen table and dropped her chin into her hand. "Aunt Lucy?"

"Yes?" She slid the steaming mug to Keisha and sat across from her.

"Where is Aunt Claire?"

I can't believe it, thought Lucy. Rasheda leaves for 5 minutes and I have to deal with this. "Have you asked your parents?"

Keisha nodded.

"What did they say?"

"Something silly." She blew on her hot chocolate. "Daddy said Aunt Claire went to sleep and won't ever wake up. But I just looked in the bedroom and she's not there."

"How about your mom?"

"Mama said Claire's in heaven with God."

Lucy regarded her silently. These were such solemn questions to emerge from a person wearing little red overalls with a purple dinosaur rearing across the chest. "Well, I think it's a little of both," she began slowly. "Claire's body got sick, so sick that she died."

"Went to sleep and didn't wake up," Keisha added helpfully.

"That's right. But her soul, her spirit"—Lucy stopped—"Do you know about souls?"

Keisha nodded.

"Well, her soul went to heaven, but it's still here too." With both hands, Lucy pressed her chest. "Claire's soul lives in my heart, and in your mama's heart, and everywhere somebody loved her."

"But how did the sickness get into her body?"

"I don't know, honey."

Keisha gulped down some cocoa. "Will you die too?"

"Well, someday, but not because of Claire. She didn't have the kind of sickness you can catch."

"Then why will you die?"

"Everybody dies. But most people don't die until they're old."

"Aunt Claire was older than Mama."

"I know. But most people don't die until they're very, very old—way older than your grandma, even."

"What about your heart?" Keisha pressed her hands against her chest with the same gesture Lucy had used. "Mama says your heart is sick."

"People sometimes say that when they mean that someone's really sad. But no one dies of sadness. They may think they're going to—they may even think they want to—but no one does."

"Oh." She tipped her mug so far back that all Lucy could see was her throat and the tiny crescent of her lower lip. "Hey, want to hear what I can play on the piano?" Keisha ran into the living room.

Following her, Lucy remembered the day they had moved into the house, more than 8 years before. "Where do you want this, lady?" the mover had asked as three men muscled the piano into the room.

"I'm not sure," Claire had replied. "Let's try it in that corner, and if it's not right, we'll put it against the wall."

"The deal is you only get one shot with pianos. My guys aren't picking it up again."

"Why didn't you mention that before they picked it up?"

"I'm mentioning it now."

"Fine," Claire had answered. "Then you can tell them to hold it until I decide."

Claire had loved Billie Holiday, Bessie Smith, the deepest blues. Now, as Lucy watched Keisha confidently pick out "Twinkle Twinkle Little Star," she thought nothing could be bluer than the unanswered refrain, *How I wonder where you are.*

"Keisha, can you play 'Mary Had a Little Lamb'?"

"Sure!" She launched into the song, her pigtails bobbing.

Lucy sat beside her on the long bench. "You look like you enjoy playing."

"It's fun."

"You don't have a piano at home, do you?"

"Daddy says we have to save up for one. He gave me a piggy bank so I can help."

Lucy stared at the keys. Of course—it was so obvious! The piano had to go. It hunkered in the living room like a huge symbol of loss. Claire had adored the piano for its strong, simple shape, its patient wood, its tolerant strings. She would not want it to sit neglected; she would want her piano to go someplace where it would be played and appreciated. Someplace like the Coopers' house.

Rasheda flung open the door. "The warrior returns with beans and bread."

"Mama, listen to me play!"

"I heard you, sweetheart, all the way up the driveway." She shrugged off her jacket. "Let's get the coffee on. I'm starving."

"Mama, can I have a bagel? I want to feed the birds."

"Sure. Here's one with poppy seeds. Birds ought to go for that in a big way." The two women watched Keisha gallop out the kitchen door. "Zip your jacket," called her mother without much hope.

"Rasheda, I had the greatest idea while you were gone." Lucy dropped a bagel into the toaster.

"What's that?"

"You have to take the piano."

"I told you we walked over. I don't think it'll fit in Keisha's backpack."

"No, I'm serious. I want you to have it."

Rasheda set down the coffeepot. "Why?"

"Keisha wants a piano, for one thing."

"Keisha is a child of the '90s. She wants everything."

"Claire loved that piano. I think it would mean a lot to her to know you're enjoying it."

"This is a big step, Lucy. Are you sure you're ready to start giving away Claire's things?"

"Rasheda, if I'm ever going to be more than a bruise with legs, I have to make a start somewhere." She smiled. "Besides, Claire's piano will be staying in the family. Doesn't Keisha think we're her aunts?"

Rasheda took her hands. "You are her aunts, and that's the straight up truth."

∞ ∞ ∞

Lucy could hardly believe how quickly it all happened. She was reminded of the magical way in which the rented hospital bed and portable toilet had vanished from the house after Claire's death.

"Now you see what they're good for." Rasheda pointed as her husband and three of his friends hefted the piano onto a padded dolly.

Lucy and Rasheda hurried into the electric fall air to kick pine cones out of the path of the rumbling dolly. Grunting in concert, they helped the men push the piano up the ramp into the rented truck. Lucy stood in the road to watch the glinting little caravan lumber down the hill and out of sight.

Inside, she walked slowly to the newly vacant corner of her living room. Imprinted on the golden oak floor was a piano-shaped shadow of darker wood. Lucy sank and pulled her knees against her chest, rocking in the space where hands would never again make music.

∞ ∞ ∞ **11** ∞ ∞ ∞

THROWING TABLES

Almost a hundred years before, Harry's office had started its life as the dining room of a dignified Victorian mansion. But the house had declined with the century, until finally it was remodeled and reborn into more modest circumstances as a parcel of office condominiums. His was a handsome space with high ceilings, tall rectangular windows, and gleaming dark floors. Everything in the room was oversized, from his heavy walnut desk to the blue leather armchairs to the long mahogany table under the bank of windows.

The office was made for large men, and Lucy was a small woman. Harry thought today she must feel even smaller, with her flimsy financial life spread out on the table for him to judge.

"Can I do it?" she asked him again.

Stalling, Harry thumbed through a pile of tax returns. "You can do it," he finally replied. "But are you sure you want to?"

Lucy nodded. "It's the first thing I've been sure of."

"But Lucy." Harry rubbed a hand over his smooth, square jaw. "You spent all those years and God knows how much money in school. You worked your fanny off. Now you've got a tenured position in a very insecure world. Why would you give that up?"

She raised her palms. "I can't do it any more, Harry. To get up in front of a classroom and talk about books . . . It's just not in me now."

Harry studied her across the expanse of wood and papers. With her back to the blazing windows, Lucy looked like a cardboard cutout. Her fine brown hair just grazed her shoulders. Her slender, folded arms and white turtleneck gave her an air of vulnerability, but her dark eyes were stubborn as stones.

He sighed. Claire had not asked him to look after Lucy, not exactly, but he had made a private vow to do so. He just hadn't anticipated how exhausted he would be when the time came. "Couldn't you take a leave of absence or something until you feel more positive?"

"I've used all the leave I'm entitled to. In fact, the university's been very generous, considering."

"Considering what?"

She pressed her lips into a thin line. "That we weren't legally married."

"Oh." Harry pulled his legal pad closer, clicked out a fresh point on his mechanical pencil. "Here's the deal. You can do it. You can quit your job and take some significant time off—several years, if you want. I could structure something for you using Claire's insurance and your savings." He looked up at her. "But then what? In 6 years you'll be out of a job, left behind in your profession, and fresh out of assets. And you'll be 50 years old."

"Harry, if I stay, 6 years from now I'll be one of those teachers who's dead in the head. And I'll still be 50 years old."

Harry scanned the tower of numbers he had constructed on his legal pad. "But you'd be abandoning the only work you've ever known. Doesn't that scare you?"

"I'm scared all the time now." Lucy leaned toward him, hands clasped in front of her on the table. "I'm getting some courage from you."

"From me?"

"You did what I'm trying to do. You left that fat-cat accounting firm in New York to move here."

"That was a whole different story." He tugged at his flowered tie. "I was the first person in my family to go to college. No one pictured any white-collar career for me."

"What did they picture?"

"They probably expected me to work in the dairy, like my dad and all his brothers. I mean, they were proud when I joined the firm, but it made a difference between us. My folks only visited me once in Manhattan. They thought it was inhabited by a race of crazy people. So when I came here to do accounting for florists and pharmacists, they were relieved. This is a way of life that makes sense to them. But if I had given up my profession and just blown off those three letters after my name?" He shrugged. "Well."

"That's what your family thought about it. What did you think?"

Harry grinned. "It scared the hell out of me. I wasn't sure I could give up the big bucks."

"Well, I won't have that problem."

"And I didn't know anyone here except you and Claire. Don't you remember?"

"How you spent every weekend cowering on our couch? No, I don't remember. But as soon as you started meeting cute young women at the health club, you were gone."

"Yeah, well. I already told you, those days are over."

"You told me, but you never told me why. Besides, I don't believe it. Things didn't work out with Cynthia, but someone else will come along. They always do."

"Whatever." Amazing how easily she dismissed his feelings. Harry tossed down his pencil. "Hey, what do you say we move this conversation to the Bean Counter? I'm ready to wrap it up here."

Fifteen minutes later, they settled at a high table in the town's newest coffee bar. Through the window to his left, he could see the steady, colorful traffic moving like a film down the broad street, with its old-fashioned pharmacy, its bicycle store, its bagel shop. In the fragile evening light, pedestrians floated past the storefront, conversing in pantomime. Their feet raised silent gusts of russet leaves.

The place sold 28 varieties of coffee from 9 countries. Lucy ordered decaf, black. If Claire were here, she and Harry would still be debating which brew to buy. They would select something exotic for each of them, and a third cup to sample. But Claire was not here. That was the point. Claire was gone, and Harry was the only one left to stop Lucy from making a terrible mistake.

Harry faced her across the narrow rectangle of hammered tin. He shifted on his tall, spindly stool; the cane seat seemed to have a body heat of its own. "So what were you thinking of doing if you left the university?"

"I'm not sure. Nothing, for a while."

"Sounds good." Harry stirred a pinch of nutmeg into his cappuccino.

Lucy gave him a sharp glance. "Are you being sarcastic?"

"No! I'm tired to my soul. I could sit in my living room and do nothing for a good long time." Here was a man who had barely slept through the night in months. Weariness oozed through his veins. He felt grit behind his eyes. How could she not know this about him? Was he invisible to her? "But then what do you want to do, after you're done doing nothing?"

"I'm not certain. But I know it has to be something very different, something removed from academia." She stared out the window, hands wrapped around her purple mug. "I think maybe I'd like to start a business of my own. Some kind of store."

Harry closed his eyes. This was worse than he thought.

"Maybe a bookstore," she continued. "That would be fun."

"We have two good bookstores in town, plus the university bookstore, and a Borders is opening in the spring. This would be a tough time to launch an independent bookstore."

"Oh. Well, my other thought was a nursery. I think it might be very satisfying to handle plants all day. Plants can't talk."

"You know, one of my clients owns a nursery. If you want, I'll introduce you to him. His bottom line doesn't look any too sturdy, but maybe he'd let you work there for a little while, see what it's really like."

"Harry, are you by any chance trying to dissuade me?"

"I'm just being realistic. You came to me for advice, and I'm giving you some. Running a retail business is damned hard work. Starting one is harder. Most don't break even for the first 5 years, and a lot of them don't make it that long. Haven't you ever noticed how many new shops and restaurants are opening all the time in Sterling? It's true the town is growing, but it's not growing that much. Most of the new businesses are replacing ones that folded."

Harry gulped back some cappuccino. He wanted to give Lucy a chance to respond, to ask questions, to defend her idea. Mainly he wanted to stop feeling like he was bullying her. But Lucy did not look intimidated, merely attentive.

"I know you work hard now," he continued, "but this is different. Dealing with the public is a particular kind of hell. Not everyone is suited for it. You'd be scrambling for bucks, teetering on a razor-thin profit margin, and paying your own taxes, insurance, everything. And you can forget about vacations, or even weekends. My clients swear their businesses own them, not the other way around."

"What would you suggest I do, then? Given the fact that life as usual is no longer an option."

"As your financial advisor, I urge you to investigate thoroughly before you make a move. Talk with business owners. Look at their books. Work somewhere for a while. Get a realistic perspective on what your daily tasks and risks would be. I can set you up with a few of my clients if you want."

She nodded. "That makes sense."

"And as your friend, I really think you should give yourself some time. Try to stay on at the university. Maybe you could convince them to grant you an extended leave without pay. I can structure your assets so you'd get a regular monthly income. But wait before you make such a big decision."

"What am I waiting for?"

He swirled the dregs of his coffee. "Well, you know all the books say not to make any major changes in your life within the first year."

"Harry, what are you doing reading up on grief?"

He spread his fingers on the tabletop and concentrated on the feel of cool metal beneath his palms. Lucy's life had been trashed, it was true. But did she have to be so blind? "I'm grieving," he replied in a dry, steady voice. "I read those books because I've lost someone, same as you." The little sandy hairs on the back of his hands looked like transplanted eyelashes. He couldn't stop staring at them. "Maybe I wasn't Claire's closest friend, but she was mine. I've had all those women in my life—sisters and girlfriends—but somehow Claire was my home base. Now she's dead, and I'm not getting over it. So I buy books." Finally he looked up at Lucy. "Did you think you were the only one?"

"I'm sorry." Lucy rested her small pale hand on top of his. "You know, I walk around stewing in all this pain, and everyone's sick of hearing about it. I'm so sunk in it I forget that other people loved her too."

"It's okay," he said gruffly.

"No, it's not. But the other thing is . . ."

"What?"

"I guess I think of you as invulnerable. If you wanted to, you could probably pick up this table and throw it across the room. And I've never seen you cry."

"That's not a sign of strength. It's more of a . . . I don't know, an absence. A lack." He thumped his chest where the burning ache resided. "I wish I could cry. I think a man who was truly strong would know how."

"Does your father know how?"

"I'm not sure. I did see him cry once. It was a long time ago, when John Kennedy was killed. That shocked me more than anything, to see my dad drop his head in his hands and weep. As far as I know, he never did it again. Never voted again, either."

Lucy slid off the high wooden stool. "If you're fully caffeinated, why don't you come over to my house for dinner? I made some really good vegetable stew over the weekend."

Harry smiled at her. "Is this a date?"

"I suppose. If we're both going to live cloistered lives, we might as well do it together."

∞ ∞ ∞

After dinner they moved to the front porch. The sharp autumn air was a thrilling liquid. Harry settled into his accustomed wicker chair and propped his long legs on the railing. "Guess we won't be sitting out here much longer."

"No, in another couple of weeks it'll be too cold."

He watched Lucy glide across the porch, pausing every few steps to light a white candle cradled in a tulip-shaped glass bowl. The glow she created felt both cozy and melancholy. "I never noticed candles before. Are those new?"

"Yes." Lucy shook out the match and sat beside him. "Claire never wanted any light out here. You know how she loved the dark."

"I know how she fantasized about shooting out the street lights with a BB gun."

Lucy laughed. "Yes, well, that's what I mean. Claire thought lighting up the porch would isolate us from the rest of the night-time world, and she was right. It feels like you and I are floating all alone on this island of amber light." She turned up the collar of her heavy denim jacket.

A car toiled up the hill and past the house, its blinker flashing. Harry could hear the slow evening traffic in the valley below, passing like breezes in the dark. "What is this like for you?" he ventured. "How do you stand it, day after day?"

Lucy drew her knees up to her chest and wrapped her arms around them. "You know, people talk about grief as if it's a wound that will heal. But a wound is specific, it's finite. This is more like . . . more like my skin's been flayed off, and I'm expected to walk around like this, and rake my leaves, and pay my bills, and say good morning to people in the grocery store."

"You told me people are sick of hearing about it. What makes you think that?"

"People say things."

"Like what?"

"Like 'It's been almost a year. What have you been doing with yourself?' Or 'Call me when you get on your feet. We'll have dinner.'"

Harry clenched his fists. "Who says those things?"

"Neighbors. Colleagues at school. Even a few of my relatives." Lucy's voice grew hard. "I bet things would be different if Claire had been a man. When my cousin Marilyn lost her husband, it was a big family tragedy. I haven't even gotten a card from Marilyn. And she's met Claire a dozen times. We drove to Boston for her wedding!

"If this is what happens to people who are out, I can't even picture what it's like for couples who are closeted. Can you imagine losing your partner and not being able to acknowledge what she meant to you? And having people ask you if you're looking for a new roommate, or if you plan to move to a smaller place?"

"Has anyone asked you that?" Harry demanded.

"No. Why? Should they?"

"Of course not."

"I mean, do you think it would be a good idea financially?"

"Hold on to the house. It's an asset." He plunked both feet on the wooden floor as if to emphasize its soundness. "Besides, so much of your life is rooted here. Every room is full of Claire. It's almost like she's about to walk in the door any minute."

"Harry, she's not."

"But what if she did? What if Claire came back and you weren't here? If there's a way to do it, Claire would figure it out."

"Oh, Harry." She shook her head. "Sometimes I think I do feel her. It's a little rush of warmth, like a breeze, only it's inside me. If Claire has a presence in this world, that's how we'll experience it. Not through real estate."

They fell silent for a few moments.

"You know, I wish you had been around more at the end," Lucy began. "That might have made it easier for you to let go."

"What do you mean? I was around."

"I know. You were here, answering the phone, bringing lunch for the hospice nurses. But in those last few days you weren't in the room with Claire. You didn't see the devastation."

But Harry had seen it. During the last week of Claire's life, he had tiptoed into her room while Lucy was somewhere else for a few moments.

He thought he knew what to expect. Claire's body was in the process of shutting down. Dwindling, the doctor had called it, and it had seemed such a gentle word. But what he found horrified him. Claire's head loomed monstrously above her shrunken neck. Her face resembled a mask made of greasy waxed paper; her jutting cheekbones practically split the skin.

She had opened her eyes for an instant, and her scabbed lips moved. "Harry," Claire whispered. "Get me out of here."

He had turned his back on Claire and bolted from the room.

And now he had to answer to Lucy for his cowardice. "I wanted to be with her." The words felt like gravel in his throat. "I just couldn't handle it."

"And you think we could? Do you think it was any easier for me? Or for Jane and Rasheda? Did you think we were any less sickened by her suffering?"

Harry planted both elbows on his knees and hung his head. "I didn't think about it like that. I only knew I couldn't do it."

"Well, let me tell you something. I couldn't do it either. But I did it. Maybe that's the difference between women and men."

He laced his fingers behind his neck and stared at the floor. Lucy was right. What good was his hard, health-club body, his toned muscles, his powerful grip?

"You spend all that time at the gym," Claire had chided him, "and then you pay someone to do your yard work. Don't you know you could be working on a good-looking body *and* a good-looking back yard, at the same time?"

"And I suppose you are a paragon of consistency," he had retorted. "You've spent the past 20 years in a TV station, and your VCR is still flashing 12:00."

"That's not the same at all," snorted Claire. "You're comparing apples and sour grapes."

What would Claire think if she could see him now, see through his burnished skin and sculpted muscles, all the way to his dry, splintery heart?

"Harry, you've got a nice house," she would say. "Too bad nobody's home."

But he could never explain this to Lucy. Lucy, who thought he could throw tables, who believed he was invulnerable. He was a lightweight compared to Lucy.

And yet he was better than most. That's what she never gave him credit for. Lots of men would have vanished at the first sign of trouble. Most guys would have given up on Claire when she started sleeping with women, or when she settled down in this lesbian love nest, or for damn sure when she came home from the

142

hospital with a prognosis that was shorter than football season.

But not Harry. When Harry loved someone, he was loyal to the end—beyond the end, even. It was just one of life's little jokes that the only women he could get close to were the kind he couldn't fuck.

Finally Lucy broke the miserable silence. "You know what would be great right now?"

"What?"

"A cigarette."

Harry peered at her. "You don't smoke."

"I used to, when I was in my twenties. It was such a comforting ritual."

"A pipe would be even better," he suggested. "All that knocking and filling and tamping. All that match-lighting."

"That would be better. Maybe you and I are destined to grow old together, sitting here on this porch, smoking our pipes."

"So, um, does this mean you accept my apology?"

She twisted in her seat so suddenly the chair thumped back and forth with the sound of a heartbeat. "Harry, for God's sake, grow up! I don't want your apology. I'm angry, okay? I know you did your best, but it wasn't enough. Not even close. But don't think you're special; I'm angry at everyone."

"Who else?"

"I'm mad at Rasheda because she wasted the last good hours she could have spent with Claire. She was working overtime, trying to save Claire's job—as if Claire was ever going back to it! Who cared if they hired someone new?"

"Insurance," Harry interrupted. "Claire could have lost her insurance."

"Claire's insurance was almost useless. You know how much home health care it provided? Five days! I'm still fighting with her insurance company."

"Anyone else?"

"I keep telling you, everyone. I'm mad at my mother because she doesn't call enough. I'm mad at Claire's mother because she calls too often. I'm angry at Jane because now that I need her, she's decided to fall in love. But mostly I'm furious at Claire for going off and leaving me in this mess. I could kill her myself!" Lucy barked out a drunken-sounding laugh.

"Lucy, have you thought about getting some help with this? Maybe you could join some kind of support group."

"Maybe I should. Then I can be mad at some strangers, too."

Hearing a jaunty "beep-beep," Harry swivelled to watch a red Jeep scoot up the hill. "Who's that?"

"That's Roxanne, Jane's girlfriend."

"I can't get used to the idea of Jane being hooked up with someone. She's the only one I could rely on to be in worse shape than I was romantically."

"Better brace yourself then," Lucy advised as the Jeep crunched to a stop.

"Hi!" called out Jane. "Is it okay for us to drop in like this? We were in the area."

"Sure. What were you doing in this neighborhood?"

They clambered onto the porch. "Roller skating!" exclaimed Roxanne. "It was a riot. I fell down so many times I probably won't be able to sit tomorrow. But it was worth it."

Harry checked her out. She was good-looking and vivacious. Not at all the serious type he had imagined for Jane. He slid his chair to make room for the two women in the ring of candlelight.

"Ah, Harry," said Roxanne when Jane introduced them. "As in, 'If only they could all be like Harry.'"

"Jane says that?"

"Indeed she does." She dragged a chair into the circle.

"Where were you, Jane, the old Rollerama on Fountain Street?" asked Lucy. "That place was ancient when we moved here. I can't believe it's still open."

"Open and thriving," Jane confirmed. "It is kind of amazing."

"Do they still have that cheesy organ music?" wondered Harry.

"Oh, no. Now they have CDs and computer programming. It's all very sophisticated."

"I guess it has to be, to attract kids."

"I suppose so. We must have been the oldest people there by at least a decade, wouldn't you say, Rox?"'

But Roxanne was not listening. She leaned close to Lucy. "I'm sitting in her chair, aren't I?"

"How'd you know?"

"The expression on your face when I sat down."

Lucy nodded. "But it's all right."

"I know. Everything belongs to her."

Lucy looked at her intently. "Have you been through this?"

"Not exactly. But I know a little about living with absence."

"What do you mean?"

"I had a partner once," Roxanne began. She glanced at Jane, who dipped her head in assent. "We were together for a long time, almost as long as you and Claire. When we split up, the rupture was total. She's still living in St. Louis, but it's as if she vanished. I never saw her again. I never heard her voice." Roxanne said all of this very carefully. Harry surmised that she had tried to explain it before and been misunderstood.

"When did this happen?" Lucy asked.

"Three years ago."

"And have you been involved with anyone since then?" She looked at Jane, who rested her fingertips on Roxanne's knee.

"I've gone out with a few women. But Jane is the first one I've wanted to see over toast and coffee."

"So it's possible to get over it," Lucy mused.

"Yes and no," Roxanne answered slowly. "I mean, your life continues. Every day spins you farther from the time you shared with her. You accumulate new experiences, new friends, new feelings. But that room is always occupied."

"I see."

"Don't get me wrong," added Roxanne. "I know it's not the same. Claire is gone, and my partner is still in the world."

Eyes glistening, Lucy reached over and took Roxanne's hand. "Not your world."

Harry watched the women, mesmerized. Here was Lucy, who could not quite countenance his own grief, moved to tears at the tale of a stranger's breakup with her girlfriend. And here was Jane, who hadn't had a date in so long you'd think she'd be a little insecure, appearing entirely at ease as Roxanne related the story of her undying love for someone else.

Women are amazing creatures, thought Harry. And nothing confirmed this better for him than spending time with lesbians. It was like observing women in the wild, unfettered by the need to please men.

All his life Harry had pursued women who needed men, who were willing to shape themselves for him, who found their whole world in his eyes. No wonder he had so often failed; the responsibility was enormous.

But maybe when he was not around, the women Harry dated behaved more like these women. Maybe they too turned every experience into a story. Perhaps they spent whole afternoons around the kitchen table with their friends, laughing so hard they began to snort. Possibly they shuffled to the coffeepot in the morning with sleep-tousled hair, wearing wrinkly pajamas and big fleecy slippers. All of these behaviors he found utterly endearing, but if the women Harry was involved with behaved that way, they kept it from him. What they hid from Harry was exactly what might have let him love them. Not one of Harry's women had allowed herself to be real with him—except Cynthia, on the day he left her.

Now the three women appeared to be silent, but Harry knew better. They were communicating on a frequency he could not hear. For the first time, he realized how smoothly Claire had translated for him. Harry dropped his head in despair at the poor, feeble language he was left with. No one looked his way. No one reached for his hand. In the dancing ring of light, he was invisible, a hunk of wood, an empty chair.

He felt a pressure squeezing his heart like a fist. It spread through his chest and into his throat. It burned behind his eyes and nose. His face buried in his hands, Harry let the sensation push through him, felt it press against his skin from the inside. It was like sex, voluptuous, inevitable. He almost groaned with the release of it.

Liquid squeezed from his eyes and splattered his lips with the taste of salt. A creaky sound twisted from his own throat. Harry's chest heaved with hoarse, rusty sobs.

He felt a woman's arm around his shoulders, another on his knee. Finally they saw him. Finally they were letting him in. But it didn't matter any more, it was too late. He had found his own way home.

THE LAPSED WORLD

Lucy felt like the priestess of some strange religion as she knelt before the glowing domestic altar, bobbing and swabbing in the familiar ritual of cleaning out the refrigerator. Surrounding her on the checkered floor stood squat, sweating jars of mustards, jams, and sauces, elegant glass cylinders of olives and capers, a bottle of tiny mushrooms floating in brine.

How had they acquired all these foodstuffs? She wondered. Lucy, who thought Dijon mustard was quite racy enough, never shared in Claire's pursuit of the most adventurous flavor. Still, she had enjoyed indulging Claire and even urging her on to see how far she would go. Pizza with goat cheese and hot peppers? Why not? One of Lucy's delights had been to journey to the Chinese market in Syracuse, where she stocked up on potent hot sauce and crinkly bags of candied ginger that Claire would munch until her mouth was on fire.

As Lucy wrung out her rag, she wondered what stories might be gleaned by studying the entrails of the refrigerator. Anyone could see that here lived a family of eclectic tastes. But could a trained observer, examining this gnawed-looking box of baking soda, surmise that Claire—who spent her days adjusting images by increments of one-thirtieth of a second—at home lacked the patience to read instructions such as "Open Here"?

The refrigerator was the pulsing heart of the kitchen, a trunk full of tiny domestic tales. As Lucy wrestled the vegetable drawer out of its housing, she remembered the time she had found Claire at the kitchen counter, struggling to open a jar of olives. Lucy had showed her how to break the vacuum by tapping the lid. Claire was as gleeful as if Lucy had taught her some esoteric secret instead of a common household tip.

Well, after today the refrigerator would tell a different story. Lucy had scrubbed down the shelves, the walls, the inside of the door. She had swept away the scatter of coffee grounds, the transparent slips of onion skin, the expired batteries that had been hiding in the butter holder. Now she plunked herself cross-legged on the floor and tossed into the trash can all the jars and bottles she would never want. Each new addition landed with a satisfying clunk.

Lucy was taking aim with a bottle of Louisiana hot sauce when the phone rang. She wiped her hands on her sweatpants.

"Hi, Lucy, what're you up to?" boomed Harry. "Getting a head start on your life of leisure?"

"Not exactly. I'm cleaning the fridge."

"Oh, do refrigerators need cleaning?"

"Of course they do."

"I don't think I've ever done that. Maybe mine is self-cleaning."

"Harry, you're scaring me." Lucy filled the tea kettle. "I've eaten dinner at your house."

"Well, how could I tell if my refrigerator needed to be cleaned?"

"You'd notice it was starting to grow fur."

"Maybe my cleaning woman does it."

"You have a cleaning woman?"

"Every 2 weeks. She's a sophomore at the university. Trying to decide whether to major in French literature or European history."

Lucy opened a cabinet and poked through boxes of tea. "What do you advise her?"

"To start a house-cleaning business. She'll make more money. Speaking of which, I'm working on your financial plan. Do you want to hang on to the vacation property?"

She chuckled. "Yes, I'll keep the vacation property, but let's liquidate the oil wells."

"Cute. But really, Lucy, have you thought about what you want to do with it?"

"What vacation property are you talking about?"

"Okay, maybe it's not vacation property. Maybe it's your little retirement nest egg. Let's see, where is it?" Lucy heard him clicking at a computer keyboard. "I'm talking about the 1.5 acres of unimproved property in the Upper Eau Claire Lakes region of Wisconsin. Do you want me to sell it, or do you think you might want to build there someday?"

She dropped a pillowy tea bag into her mug. "Harry, I've never even been to Wisconsin. We don't own any property there."

"Well, I sure hope you do, because Claire's been paying taxes on it for 5 years."

"Five years!" Lucy sat down, hard, on a bentwood chair. "I don't understand."

"Are you telling me you don't know anything about this?"

"No, nothing. Harry, there must be some mistake. Claire doesn't own any land."

"I'm sorry, Lucy, but she does. She did. Now you own it."

"Well, when did she buy it? What for?" Lucy's gaze darted around the kitchen. The high white ceiling, the tawny wooden cabinets, the scratched oak table were suddenly unfamiliar. "Why didn't she tell me?"

"I don't know. I always assumed you had bought it together."

"You must have some kind of papers there. A receipt, or a deed or something."

"No, I just handled the taxes. The papers would probably be somewhere in the house. Have you gone through her desk yet?"

She pressed her fingertips against her closed eyes. "No. It felt like such an invasion."

"Lucy, it's important for you to take charge of Claire's estate. You can't leave it all for the lawyer and me to handle indefinitely. Do you want me to come over and help you look through her stuff?"

"I don't think so. Harry, why would she want a secret homestead in Wisconsin?"

"We don't know that it was a homestead. It's just land—no buildings, no improvements. Maybe she wanted to own a little chunk of the forest while there was still some left. Maybe it was an investment."

"An investment! Claire didn't even like to buy bananas that weren't ripe yet."

"I know."

"Harry, something is wrong here."

"Let's not jump to conclusions, Lucy. It could be something perfectly benign. Sorry—that was a bad choice of words."

"But if it was so benign, why didn't Claire tell me about it?"

Harry only sighed. "Look, call me as soon as you find the papers."

Lucy hung up. Head in her hands, she ignored the hissing tea kettle. The sound sharpened into a whistle that climbed and climbed until it became a shriek. How much louder could it get, Lucy wondered, before the dull silver kettle exploded, flinging homely fragments everywhere? How much longer could it replicate the howling inside her?

She lunged to the stove and twisted the knob. The shriek subsided into ringing silence.

"What's the worst that could happen?" Claire used to ask, and then it had happened. There were stories Lucy would never tell Claire: some stories still untapped from their years together, and every story from now on. Even worse were the questions Claire would never be able to answer, questions profound and trivial that nattered in Lucy's head like a radio left on in a vacant house. If you had known how soon your life would end, would you have lived differently? What were your last thoughts? Have you seen the red screwdriver? Was I able to make you certain, deep down in your bones, that I cherished you? Was it ever enough?

And now this, thought Lucy, trudging up the stairs to the bedroom. A conundrum straight out of a soap opera.

She paused in the doorway and surveyed the large rectangular room. At the far end, the blue-quilted bed stood between two tall, shuttered windows. Closer to Lucy, Claire's desk nestled into a dormer cut in the sloping roof. The burled maple was silky to the touch; the seven drawers with their smooth, incised handles glided silently. Lucy knew this because she and Claire had bought the desk at a huge outdoor auction when they first moved to Sterling.

Since then, Lucy had not found cause to open the drawers. She had her own study in the next room; it seemed the least she could do to respect the privacy of Claire's desk. Even now, as she pulled up the pine folding chair, Lucy felt sick with disloyalty. Holding her breath, she slid open the slim center drawer.

Gingerly, she picked through the items. Yellow-bodied pencils and ball-point pens. Old, cracking rubber bands. A pack of index cards held together with an elastic hair tie. Loose stamps, some tarnished pennies, a pencil sharpener shaped like a shoe. A cluster of keys, unlabeled. Did one of them unlock the cabin in Wisconsin? But Harry had said there was no cabin, only land. Land that Claire had bought—handing over the check furtively, or matter-of-factly, or with a great grin of triumph—to escape from a life Lucy had believed she loved. Or did Lucy merely assume Claire was happy because she herself was so content?

Most evenings Claire would come home from work and noodle out some blues on her piano. Sometimes when the two of them argued, she would dissolve Lucy's resistance by quavering "Oh, Rob!" just like Mary Tyler Moore. Every now and then she lit candles and entreated Lucy to dance in the darkened living room. Were these the actions of a woman who was planning to flee?

Lucy shoved the drawer closed and drew open the next. Boxes of unused checks. A chrome stop watch, a stack of Post-it notes. Three rolls of pennies. A collection of felt-tip pens, clumped together with a rubber band. An address book. In the back corner of the drawer, a curled photograph. Lucy hesitated. Did she really want to learn whatever it was Claire had kept from her? She closed her eyes and brought the photo into the light.

It was a picture of Lucy herself. She was stepping out of the bathroom, a blue towel wrapped around her body, another piled like a turban on her head. On her face was a silly expression of surprise that only someone who loved her would find endearing.

She yanked out the remaining drawers and dumped them onto the wooden floor. The deed to their own house Lucy remembered as a thick packet of long white paper, folded into a light blue cover. She didn't know if she was looking for something similar, but whatever it was, she needed to find it quickly. Lucy pawed through the heap of papers, bills, canceled checks, unused envelopes, old post cards. Claire's beautiful desk looked like a face with its teeth knocked out, but Lucy didn't care.

She dragged the chair over to the closet. Those high shelves where Claire so sweetly offered to stack Lucy's off-season garments could serve as a perfect hiding place. Claire might even have stashed whatever it was among Lucy's own clothing.

She patted down her own t-shirts and shorts. Nothing. Rifling through Claire's folded sweaters and shirts, Lucy felt a surge of panic. She hurled the clothing to the floor to see if a deed, a photo, a love letter might flutter out.

Lucy was panting now, her pulse banging in her temples. Where else would Claire hide things? Where did Claire go that she did not? Knocking over the chair, she jumped to the littered floor and hurtled down the stairs to the kitchen.

The top row of cupboards! Lucy never used them, had barely even looked up there since she laid down shelf paper years ago. She wedged a chair against the counter and climbed up, swinging the doors wide. It occurred to her that Claire *would* die if she could see Lucy teetering with her filthy sneakers on the kitchen counter.

Lucy shoved aside the front row of boxes and jars, but she still couldn't see the shadowy shapes in the back of the deep cabinet. One hand clutching the shelf for balance, she plunged her arm into the darkness and swept the whole collection onto the floor, cringing at the shattering of glass, the tattoo of rice raining down. Nothing mattered but to find the secret, the clue, the answer to the riddle, whatever it was, however awful. She inched her way down the counter to the next cupboard and emptied it. Somewhere in here, somewhere amidst the chunky health food cereals and the cups of instant noodles and the petrified cubes of bouillon hid the key that would reveal whether Claire had gone to her grave a stranger.

Lucy knew it was ridiculous. No one would hide evidence of a sordid secret life behind popcorn oil and bags of carob chips. But she couldn't stop herself. She was almost crying, gasping in ragged little breaths with a high-pitched catch in each one. Gripping the cabinet with numb fingers, her bent knees trembling, Lucy could feel her whole self ballooning with desperation. She had just enough presence of mind left to realize, with awe, that she was hysterical. Lucy had always thought hysteria was a myth, like love at first sight or Pandora's box. Now she knew herself to be irretrievably out of control. With a sob of exertion, she dashed the contents of the last shelf onto the pile below her.

Lucy had found nothing, destroyed everything. In despair, she scanned the dim, empty shelves, waiting for a burst of adrenaline to tell her what to do next. A square of whiteness caught her eye. She stood on her tiptoes, stretched her unsteady hand into the far corner to reach the clue that would explain everything. She drew it forward and stared.

It was a packet of hot chocolate. With marshmallows. With a cry, Lucy hurled it into the sink. Her fingers lost their grip on the shelf; her sneakers slipped off the edge of the counter with a sound like a rubber band snapping.

Incredibly, she had plenty of time to think on the way down. Lucy remembered falling down as a child. She remembered falling off bicycles, out of trees, off the roof of the garage. She remembered sliding off the shoulders of her older brother as they peeked at Christmas presents hidden in their parents' closet. It was not the sound of her fall but her own giggles that had gotten them caught. But she was no longer a child, and her fall tonight would be no laughing matter.

Lucy slammed into the floor in a flurry of flour and oatmeal. Dazed, she sat still, head hanging, waiting to discover her injuries. But aside from an aching tailbone, she could fine none. The dried goods must have broken her fall. Lucy glanced at her stinging hands to find them prickled with tiny berries of blood where broken glass had pierced the skin. On her ankle was a horizontal cut so straight it could have been scored with a ruler.

She grabbed the sink, hauled herself up and rinsed her hands. The dots of blood kept reappearing. Holding a wet a paper towel to her ankle, Lucy hobbled into the living room. Puffs of flour rose from her clothes. She pulled a cushion off the couch and, wincing, eased herself onto the floor. With shaky hands Lucy reached for the phone and punched in the familiar numbers.

"Edit suite."

"Rasheda?"

"Lucy, what's wrong?"

"Rasheda, I need help. Can you come over?"

"I'll be right there. Twenty minutes, half an hour tops."

Lucy stared at her palms, dotted with 3-dimensional freckles. At each tiny puncture a ball of blood grew slowly, almost imperceptibly, each drop perfectly spherical and balanced. It was wondrous, really, what the human body could do. She glanced at her ankle.

Once so tidy, the cut had given way to uneven rivulets of red that trailed into her sneaker.

Her heart beat extraordinarily fast, yet after each beat stretched an eternity. Between the chaos of the last hour and the comfort of Rasheda's arrival lay an oasis of peace, measured by the rhythm of her own heart. Lucy closed her eyes and exulted in the lapsed world between each beat.

∞ ∞ ∞

Not until Rasheda snapped on the living room light did Lucy notice that dusk had fallen.

"What's going on, Lucy?" Rasheda tossed her big leather bag into a chair. "Are you hurt?"

"No."

Rasheda squatted beside her. "You're bleeding!"

"I have a couple of cuts, that's all. Rasheda, do you know anything about Wisconsin?"

"We'll talk about the Dairy State later. Let me clean off this blood." She headed for the kitchen.

"Rasheda, wait—"

"Sweet Jesus! What happened here?"

"I was looking for something," Lucy replied meekly.

"Well, I sure hope it was the winning lottery ticket." Lucy heard footsteps crunching, water running, a drawer opening and closing. "Your kitchen looks like Keisha and three of her friends played in there for a week." Rasheda patted Lucy's palms and ankle with a damp towel.

"Upstairs is worse," Lucy admitted.

"What is this all about?" She sat cross-legged on the floor next to Lucy.

"Rasheda, I need you to be honest with me."

She nodded.

"Harry told me that for 5 years, Claire has owned some property in Wisconsin. Do you know anything about it?"

"No. What kind of property?"

"Just some land, up in the North Woods or somewhere. Rasheda, she never told me a thing about it. Why would anyone buy an acre and a half of land, and pay taxes on it for 5 years, and never do anything with it as far as I know, and not tell her partner? You spent every day with Claire. What was she hiding from me? Was she planning to move away? Was there someone else?"

Rasheda unzipped her leather jacket, settled her hands on her hips. "I want us to be crystal on this point, Lucy. The woman adored you. It was sickening how much she adored you. And let's get real: between the days she spent with me and the nights she spent with you, when would Claire have found time to be stepping out?"

Lucy dropped her forehead in her hand. "I know, I know. It doesn't make sense. But neither does this property. What did she want it for? How could she afford it?"

"How much did it cost?"

"I don't know. I can't find the paperwork. And Harry only did the taxes, so he doesn't know anything about the purchase either."

"Well, he can figure it out from the tax payment. Or he can call the county. You can get all kinds of information about that piece of land from the county government."

"But they can't tell me what was in Claire's mind. And that's what I need to find out."

"I know." Rasheda rested her hand on Lucy's knee. "We can find out about the transaction tomorrow. You know Harry; he's probably called already. And right now we can rule out a few possibilities." She ticked them off her fingers. "Number one, Claire was having an affair. There's just no way, and there's just no time. Number two, she planned to run away and live in the woods. Now come on, Lucy. If that property didn't have a house with heat, air conditioning, and cable, can you imagine Claire holing up there?"

Lucy smiled. "I guess not."

"Okay. So what are the other possibilities? Maybe she was going to surprise you. Maybe she was going to save up some money and build a little vacation cabin there for the two of you. Is that possible?"

"I don't know. Maybe. But Rasheda, Claire knew she was dying and she never mentioned it. Don't you think that's . . . suspicious? I mean, why would she keep it secret if it wasn't a big deal?"

She shrugged. "Maybe *because* it was no big deal. Maybe it just slipped her mind because it was so unimportant."

"Well, how did she come up with the money? A plot of land has to be expensive."

"You don't know that. Listen, Kevin and I have friends in Washington who just bought their first house. It cost $100,000 and it's barely livable. Think what that amount of money would buy here."

"A mansion."

"Right. So for all we know, an acre of land with nothing on it in Nowheresville, Wisconsin, could cost about what you're going to have to bribe me to help you pick up this mess."

Lucy sighed. "Could you just move in with me and keep me sane for the next couple of years?"

Rasheda hooked her thumb toward the kitchen. "Not the way you keep house."

Armed with brooms and dustpans, they started the clean-up. "Remember when you said Claire was the mayor of heaven?" asked Lucy as she poured a rattling pan of debris into the garbage can.

"Sure."

"What do you think heaven is like?"

Rasheda was silent as she swiped at stubborn shards of glass. "The way I think about it, heaven is more like a state than a place," she began. "When we go there, I believe we'll all exist as souls, in an atmosphere of pure love. And it won't make any difference if you're black or white, female or male, fat or thin, because we won't have any bodies.

"I'll be with my mother again, and you'll be with Claire, and best of all, we'll all be with God. But it won't matter who we were in this life, if we were lovers or neighbors or total strangers. Because we'll all be surrounded by God's love, and we'll experience such love and acceptance for one another that you and I here in this kitchen tonight can't even imagine it."

Lucy had stopped sweeping and was staring at Rasheda. She ached to feel some of the conviction that lit up the younger woman's face. But Lucy had never been able to develop any encompassing faith in a world beyond this one. To try to manufacture it now, when she was so needy, seemed fraudulent, an act of desperation. She lifted her broom.

"What do you think it's like?" asked Rasheda.

"Heaven?"

"Right."

Lucy shook her head. "I don't know. I only hope it's less lonely than here."

"It will be," she replied. "Count on it."

Lucy concentrated on her work, noting the scratching sound of glass scraping against linoleum, the tiny whirlwinds of flour created by the broom. "You know, finding out this blank space, this enigma about Claire . . . it's almost like losing her again," she mused.

"People think you only lose your loved ones when they die, but that's not true. You lose them over and over."

"What do you mean?" Rasheda hefted the bulky garbage bag and twisted a tie around its neck.

"Well, I've lost Claire . . . let's see, I can't count how many times. Even before she died. The first time was when we got the diagnosis." Lucy leaned on the broom handle. "We were sitting side by side in these round leather chairs, facing the doctor. When she said the words 'breast cancer,' I felt this actual physical impact. There was a vacuum, as if everyone on earth had gasped at once and sucked all the air out of the world. I turned to look at Claire and it took forever before she looked back at me. And that's when it hit me for the first time that this was something that was happening to Claire alone, not to us.

"The second time was months later, after Claire had undergone all the treatment and nothing had worked. We were in Connie Walker's office. I'll never forget this. Connie reached across the cluttered desk with her empty hand and said, 'I want to save you, Claire. But I can't.'"

Rasheda shivered.

"And then I lost her again in December, a few days before she died. They leave you before you expect it."

"Who?"

"Dying people. They turn away from you. It was as if Claire was already busy with something else."

"She was," said Rasheda. "She was getting to know God."

"You think?"

"I'm sure of it."

Lucy stared out the dark kitchen window. "And then we all lost her. You remember, you were here. Have you ever felt anything as vacant as Claire's body after she left it?"

"I know. I was holding her hand, and I could feel the cold seeping down her arm."

"So to find out that I didn't really know her after all . . . well, it's another one of those losses you think you'll never be able to survive."

Rasheda snapped open a garbage bag. "You know, there are corners of Kevin I'll never see no matter how long we're married. The fact is, he'll never entirely know me, I'll never entirely know Keisha. . . . I may never know everything about myself, even. Close as people can get to one another, we just don't know everything. I think that's God's way."

"God's way of doing what?"

"Keeping us interested. I mean, Claire was a charmer, no doubt about it. She could tell you to go to hell in such a way that you'd be looking forward to the journey. I spent over 40 hours a week with her, and half the time I didn't know what was going to come out of her mouth. Did you?"

"Not always."

"That's my point. A little uncertainty is a good thing. It doesn't mean you didn't know Claire. It means she was unknowable, like all humans."

"But it still nags at me." Lucy resumed sweeping. "What did she want that land for?"

"I know you're not going to let it rest. I fully expect you to grill everyone who's ever met Claire."

"So you can predict my moves."

"I never would have guessed you'd go on a rampage like this."

"No, neither would I."

"Well, you're going to be one hurtin' person tomorrow, that's for sure. You better treat yourself to a long, hot bath."

Later that night, Lucy watched the scented bubbles sink into the hot, flat bath water. Her body was a montage of unconnected parts: floating breasts, the twin islands of her kneecaps, and far away, a pair of bony feet pressed against the curved porcelain of the old clawfooted tub. She remembered the books of mix-and-match figures she had loved as a child. The picture on each page was cut into three horizontal strips, and by mixing up the strips you could create all sorts of images—a bald man wearing a ballerina's tutu over a cowboy's spurred boots.

Perhaps Claire was herself such an assemblage. Closing her eyes, Lucy could conjure up each detail: Claire's broad feet; her long, strong legs with the freckles hidden behind her knees; the flat plane of her thighs; the triangular thatch of dense hair; her jutting hip bones and tucked-in waist; her small breasts; Claire's sharp collarbone; her rounded shoulders; her warm arms, her deft hands, her easy smile; her radiant brown eyes; the way her eyebrows quirked upward when she laughed; her wild curly hair. All deeply familiar and dearly cherished.

But what did that add up to? What was it, exactly, that Lucy had loved during all those years of intimacy? A collection of habits, of sayings, of facial expressions, of behaviors. A gift, wrapped around a heart of mystery. That was all she would ever know of Claire.

∞ ∞ ∞ **13** ∞ ∞ ∞

TAKING FLIGHT

Jane hated the world from the moment her bare feet hit the cold, tiled floor of the bathroom. Four-thirty in the morning was no time to wake up; it was more like a time to go to bed. True, until Roxanne had come along, Jane hadn't seen 4:30 a.m. from either end of her day for years. Still, at this dismal hour, everything on earth looked as awful as the sleep-wrinkled face scowling at her from the mirror.

In the shower, hot water sluicing down her back, Jane reviewed the day's schedule. At 5:30, she would pile into Lucy's salt-ravaged brown Datsun, and the two of them would head for the airport. They'd catch a 7:30 flight to Chicago, where they'd change planes and fly to Eau Claire, Wisconsin. There they'd rent a car and drive north to some unpronounceable street in a small town, where a woman from the realty company would draw them a map to Claire's little piece of the forest. All to reach yet another part of the world where Claire could not be found.

Jane couldn't imagine what Lucy hoped to see there. Yet, as she pulled a large, striped towel from the rack, Jane reflected that she was glad to be going. No, that was not quite accurate: she was pleased Lucy had asked her to go, and relieved that she could finally do something to help Lucy through her misery.

Dry, dressed, and almost warm again, Jane pulled a brush through her wavy blonde hair, still damp and obedient from the shower. She tossed the brush into her overnight bag and zipped it closed.

In her lightless living room, Jane stood at the window to watch for Lucy. She saw her neighbor, Karen, emerge into the frost to run with her huge white Samoyed. The dog looked like a bounding snow bank, emitting clouds of steam as it tossed its handsome head. Jane watched the last few stars evaporate from the sky. She saw the silvery rods of headlights lance through the gray street and illuminate her driveway.

"Hi." Jane tucked her suitcase next to Lucy's in the back seat.

"Hi, yourself." Bundled in her navy parka, Lucy looked pallid in the green dashboard light.

Jane picked up a warm, white paper bag from the passenger seat. "What's this?"

"I brought some muffins for the plane."

"Good. I couldn't eat any breakfast. Too early." She clicked her seat belt into place.

"Me too." Lucy hooked her hand behind the passenger seat and, peering over her shoulder, backed out of the driveway.

The ride to the airport was mostly silent, which suited Jane fine. They rolled past the serene campus, through the dim, barely stirring town, into the hilly farmland. After several miles the road flattened out, and they sped past a flock of low warehouses that offered self-storage lockers, expert car repair, and discount linoleum. Accompanied only by the racket of the heater, the two women drove on, beyond the industrial parks and the empty lots whose owners would build to suit, all the way to the brightly lit billboard that proclaimed, improbably, 'Welcome to Sterling International Airport.'

The airport tower beckoned like a lighthouse as Lucy nosed the car into a parking slot. When she turned off the engine, the abrupt silence beat in Jane's ears. Bags dangling from their shoulders, the two women crunched across the asphalt in the weird artificial dawn of the airport's lights. Jane realized she was shivering. Soon it would snow, and then it would be Thanksgiving, and then Christmas, and then Claire would have been dead for a year. From now on, it would be cold for a long, long time.

The terminal was chilly and bright, with a shadowless, fluorescent light that seemed to banish the passing of time. Only a few passengers hurried down the gleaming hallways, their wheeled bags rumbling behind them. Behind the ticket counters, employees prepared for the day.

Lucy scanned the video display for their flight number. "Let's go right to our gate and check in. I didn't get us seat assignments."

"Lucy, we're way too early. No one will be at the gate yet. If you want to check in, we can do it at the ticket counter."

"Okay."

They lined up behind two other passengers, one of whom was slowly explaining some complicated matter to the ticket agent. The man had an accent Jane couldn't identify. His voice droned on in a soothing monotone. Every few seconds, the red-haired woman behind the counter dipped her head and said, "Uh-huh," as if she were totally engrossed in his story. Jane felt as if she could doze off standing right there in line. When Lucy clutched her arm, she jumped.

"You're going to kill me," said Lucy.

"Why?"

"I've changed my mind."

Jane tumbled the sounds in her mind, trying to sort them into a pattern that made sense. It sounded like Lucy had said, 'I've changed my mind,' but that couldn't be right. For one thing, this plan to visit Claire's land seemed to animate Lucy as nothing else had for months. For another, here they were, waiting in line to get their seat assignments. What could Lucy have said? 'I've aged in kind'? 'I may in time'?

"Hmm," Jane replied.

"That's it? That's all you have to say?" Lucy released her grip.

"Well, I don't have a strong opinion on that."

"How can you stand there and say you have no opinion at a time like this?"

Busted, thought Jane. "The thing is, I don't think I heard you correctly. What did you say?"

"I said, how can you tell me you have no opinion."

"No, before that."

"I've changed my mind. I can't go."

"Oh! Why not?"

"Because I can't violate Claire like that."

"How would going to see Claire's land violate her?" Jane was surprisingly thrilled that the trip might be cancelled, and just as surprisingly dismayed, and tingling all over with the conviction that she and Lucy were about to cross some threshold.

"I don't think I can explain it."

"Lucy, you told me these tickets are nonrefundable."

"I know. But for a fee, I can exchange them for tickets to somewhere else. Maybe I'll go to Cincinnati to see my parents or something. Here, give me your ticket."

"Are you sure?"

"I'm positive."

Jane wandered a few feet away to scan the newspapers displayed in a row of red vending machines. Here at the International Airport you could take your pick of the Sterling *Daily News*, *The New York Times*, or a glossy publication entitled *Sterling Homes on Parade*. Did anyone really believe that people might be moved to buy a house as they idled away the time before their flights? She supposed stranger things had happened. Lucy cancelling this trip, for example.

A few moments later, Lucy strode over to Jane. "I need some coffee."

"Did they let you exchange the tickets?"

"It's settled."

A few other people were already scattered around the coffee shop, sleepy-eyed travelers stoking themselves up for early flights. Jane and Lucy sat at a small round table near a huge picture window. They busied themselves with spreading their jackets on the back of their chairs, whisking crumbs off the table, placing their order. Not until her fingers were wrapped around the thick, white crockery cup did Jane speak.

"Lucy, why did you decide not to go?"

"Because it suddenly struck me how much Claire would have hated it."

"Why would she have hated it?"

Lucy blew on her coffee. "You know Claire. She liked to have a sense of control."

"I always told her she should get a job moonlighting as a dominatrix."

"Well, I don't know about that." Lucy smiled in a way that made Jane wonder if maybe she did.

"Okay, so Claire was bossy," pressed Jane. "What does that have to do with this land in Wisconsin?"

"When Claire got sick, she realized pretty quickly that the cancer was in charge. By the end, Claire was no longer in control of anything—her time, her privacy, her bodily functions. All the tiny, trivial decisions that people make every minute—what to do this afternoon, when to turn over in bed, what to have for lunch—even those were taken away from her. But there was one thing Claire kept. She kept this secret. And maybe it would be wrong for me to snatch it from her now, even though I could."

Lucy glanced down at her cup. "Or at least I think I could," she added in a small voice. "I think I could go there, and see the land, and ask around, and maybe figure out if Claire was planning to leave me, or what. But I won't."

Jane stared at the round, plastic table top, with its faint cross-hatching, as if someone had forgotten to remove the graph paper before brushing on the veneer. Lucy's argument almost made sense, but not quite. Of course, making a pilgrimage to this unknown piece of land had never exactly made sense, either. "Lucy, what in the world makes you think Claire wanted to leave you?"

"Look around, Jane. She's gone."

"Yes, but it's not as if she left you to take up with some 20-year-old ski instructor in Vermont. Claire died. It wasn't her choice."

"I know that. Don't you think I know that? I didn't say it was rational; I said she left me. And she did."

Jane turned toward the window. Outside, the sky slowly grew paler, not as if the sun was about to emerge over the earth's rim, but as if some darker pigment was leaking out of a tiny rip in the lower left-hand corner of the night. In the pinkish light of the runway, small trucks scooted across the tarmac. A tractor, towing carts filled with luggage, trundled past a parked commuter plane and out of sight.

"What was it like for her, carrying that secret?" Lucy mused. "I wonder if it was a burden."

"My guess is she just forgot about it." Jane took a last sip of her coffee.

"Secrets." Lucy plopped the bag of muffins on the table, where it sat unopened. "I hate them. I feel like I'm dragging around a secret of my own right now."

"What's that?"

"My amputated life. The one I had with Claire."

"How is that a secret?"

"Well, not to you, but to everyone I meet from now on. For instance, we have a new letter carrier on our street. She rang the doorbell the other day. When I introduced myself, I wanted to say, 'It's not what you think. There used to be a family at this address.' But she just looked at me as if I was a whole person. She couldn't see my amputated limbs."

"But Lucy, you are a whole person."

Lucy pressed her lips together. "I guess you can't see them either."

Jane leaned back in her chair as the waitress re-filled their cups and dropped a scribbled check on the table. "Lucy, do you remember Andrea?"

"That furniture mogul you used to date?"

"I went out with her three times. I'm not sure that qualifies for 'used to date.'"

"What made you think of her?"

"I was thinking about this party I went to with her. It was a Sunday brunch, at the home of one of her rich friends. I remember it was a spring morning, and the atmosphere was all very lovely and light-hearted, but as the day wore on I grew more and more chilled."

"Why?"

"Well, for one thing, Andrea's friends treated me like some sort of mascot. 'So you're Andrea's new flame. Oh, you teach *deaf* students. How *won*derful.'"

"You got the feeling that maybe you weren't the first of Andrea's mascots they'd met?"

"Yes, and that they didn't expect me to last until the next soiree."

"And did you?"

"No. But the point is, here were all these middle-aged lesbians, all of them confident and successful businesswomen, and most of them were still not out to their parents! They were talking about how awkward it was at family events, and worrying about how to introduce their partners, and . . . oh, you know, the whole repertoire of closeted behaviors. And not one of these women dared to contribute to a lesbian cause or participate in a lesbian organization."

"They may have had their reasons," Lucy pointed out.

"I'm sure they did. But I was bowled over by the weight these women carried, the way it circumscribed their lives. The weariness of keeping that secret."

"It's like all those Jane Austen characters, where you want to shake them by the shoulders and scream, 'Just tell the truth, for God's sake!'"

Jane smiled. "Did you share this with your classes when you taught Austen?"

"I didn't have to. Usually one of the students brought it up. But think about it, Jane. You'd never keep some big, fat secret from me, would you? You'd never look up and say, 'Oh, by the way, have I ever mentioned that I used to be one of the Manson girls?'"

Jane felt her heart wrench to a stop. In all this chatter about other people's secrets, she had forgotten about her own. She and Lucy had reached it: the borderline Jane had sensed them approaching from the moment Lucy capsized their plans. Amidst the coffee cups and the sugar packets, she felt their friendship teetering.

"I might keep a secret from you," Jane spoke slowly, "and in fact, I have."

Lucy hugged herself. "Is it about Claire?"

"No, it's about me. But Claire knew it."

"What is it?"

"I'm losing my hearing." There. It was out. It was out, and at that instant Jane could not remember why she had fought to keep it a secret. Lightheaded with relief, she blundered ahead. "Or at any rate, I might be losing my hearing. You know my father was deaf? Well, I have the same condition, only it's progressing much more slowly. That's how I met Roxanne—she was the doctor who diagnosed me."

"Oh, Jane." Lucy took her hand. "I'm so sorry. How long do you have? I mean, how long might it take until you, you know, lose your hearing completely?"

Jane drew her hand away and drained her coffee. It was not as if she wanted to grow deaf, yet it annoyed her no end when hearing people—people who had no connection to the deaf world and knew nothing of its richness—acted like going deaf was the worst thing on earth.

"I might not lose it completely. Roxanne thinks I might just stay where I am, at the 'pardon me?' stage. But if I do become deaf, it will be a slow process."

"Why didn't you tell me?" asked Lucy.

"I found out right before Claire got sick. She pretty much forced me to get a hearing test, at this little place in the mall. The test showed a hearing loss. I asked Claire to keep it private, and she did. I was planning to go to a real doctor, but then Claire was diagnosed and everything got so crazy. So I didn't really pin it down until this summer. And by then it seemed like we all had enough to deal with."

"That must have been an awful thing to carry around."

"Well, yes and no." Jane waited for a rumbling plane to taxi past the window. "I mean, I'm scared of becoming deaf. I don't want it to happen. On the other hand, I'm more prepared than most people. I have deaf friends, I sign, and I grew up with a deaf parent. But then, I've seen how deafness can pry people apart."

"What do you mean?"

"It messed up my parents pretty well. My mother never could accept my father's deafness. She didn't bother to learn to sign, just relied on me to serve as the translator."

"Sounds like a healthy situation."

Jane shrugged. "Silence became like a member of my family. It practically had its own place at the dinner table. And then there's the fact that I don't have any siblings. I mean, this was the 1950s. Could my mother have been the only Catholic woman in America who found the rhythm method effective?" Or had a different kind of silence descended on her parents, wondered Jane, in the one place where no words were needed?

"Did you ever ask them about that?"

"No. They weren't big on questions." Toying with a packet of sugar, Jane traced the vertical lines on the table top. In a funny way, making room for her parents' silence had helped to prepare her for Claire's death. Maybe that was why she had not been surprised to discover the tremendous amount of space Claire's absence took up.

"Is there anything I should do differently, now that I know?" Lucy asked.

"Yes. You can look at me when you speak. The visual cues help me figure out what you're saying."

"And should I start learning to sign?"

Jane tilted her head. "You'd do that for me?"

"Of course."

"Don't start practicing quite yet. I'll let you know."

"So is it still a secret?"

"I suppose not. What's weird is, I almost feel like it was a secret I was keeping from myself."

"Funny how that works sometimes." Lucy took a deep breath, let it out slowly. "I wonder what Claire was keeping from herself."

Jane glanced at the check. "What will you do with that plot of land, now that you've decided not to go there?" She laid some bills on the table.

"Sell it, I guess."

"Sight unseen?"

"Yes." Lucy nodded. "I'll leave Claire that little bit of dignity."

"You know what Claire would say if she were here?"

Lucy smiled. "She'd say, 'Get rid of your scruples, Lucy. They're in the way.' And then she'd be on that plane."

"That's about right."

Lucy pointed out the window. "Look, Jane. There goes our flight."

At the far end of the tarmac, a silver vessel gathered speed and sliced into the air. Watching it soar, Jane imagined she could rise into the sky herself, so liberated did she feel. She had uttered her secret, and nothing awful had happened. Jane squinted as the glinting airplane merged into the brightening sky. This had been the longest day, and it was still first thing in the morning.

GONE TOO SOON

The group was called "Gone Too Soon." Lucy cringed every time she thought of it. Why did a bereavement group need a title, anyway? What were they going to do, print t-shirts? She supposed it was to differentiate this group, designed for people under 50, from those for older people, which presumably sported names such as "Gone Right on Time."

Lucy tapped her fingers on the steering wheel and squinted through the dusk at the house, a large, fussy-looking Victorian. Knee-high lamps marked a curving path to the front door. A brass lantern spread a welcoming glow across the wraparound porch. The house lights were on, the shades drawn. No clues there.

Despite the advice of Sarah and others, Lucy had not researched this group in the slightest. She had seen a notice in the local paper, called the number, and left a message on the answering machine describing her situation and saying that she planned to attend. Lucy's decision to participate had been impetuous, and she feared that the need for any preparation would shatter her resolve.

As a result, all Lucy knew was that the woman who lived here was named Marina. Her husband, Fred, had been killed in a small plane crash almost 2 years earlier. So Marina had not watched illness ravage and break him, thought Lucy. She wondered if that was better. On the other hand, they'd had no time to say goodbye. What if Marina hadn't bothered to get up with him that final morning as he packed for his flight? What if they had quarreled, as couples do, knowing they'd have plenty of time to make it up?

Did Lucy really want to know what their last morning was like? Did she want to sit in a circle with a bunch of strangers who had nothing in common but their suffering? She reached for the stick shift, then hesitated. The truth was, Lucy had nothing in common with anyone—not with her friends, papering over Claire's absence with their busy-ness; not with her colleagues, swept up in the demands of a new school year; not with her family, tongue-tied and solicitous. Not even with herself, a woman who had once had energy and interests and attachments, a woman who had never dreamed she would find herself floating aimlessly, tethered to earth only by the accidental fact that her heart still pumped.

So why not? Why not march up those steps and join that group of strangers whose spouses were gone too soon? After all, talking to Aunt Stella a few weeks ago had been the deepest comfort Lucy had felt in months. She pocketed her keys and started up the walk.

Lucy had envisioned a handful of people gathered around the fire in a cozy living room, boxes of tissues tucked discreetly among the house plants. Instead, with a tight smile and a brief handshake, Marina led her into a huge white kitchen whose pristine counters and stainless steel appliances called to mind an operating room. The meeting had been set for 7 o'clock, Lucy was sure; yet from the grim faces and drained coffee cups of the six people hunched around the long white table, it was clear the discussion had begun some time earlier.

"Please sit down." Marina settled at the head of the table, and pointed to a seat beside her. Lucy balanced on the edge of the white mesh chair. "Lucy, I'm afraid we have some bad news for you."

She suppressed an urge to giggle. Everyone in this room had already heard the worst news there was. What could these strangers possibly have to tell her? Lucy gazed around the table at the four men and two other women who appeared to be so engrossed in fiddling with their cake plates and coffee cups. She turned to Marina, whose short blonde hair and green eyes glinted back at her, impenetrable as armor. "Well, what is it?" prompted Lucy.

Marina's red nails flickered like candle flames against the white lacquered table top. "Lucy, this group is for people who have lost their spouses. Married people; widows and widowers. I'm not sure you'd be comfortable here."

"I see." Lucy felt a clump of ice form and swell in her chest. Tiny hairs rose on her arms. "You're concerned about my comfort. Marina, let me ask you something. How long were you and Fred married?"

"Six years."

"Six years." Lucy nodded. "Claire and I were together for twelve. We shared our home, our lives, our families, our finances. In what way were we not married?"

Marina glanced at the others as if for help, but they sat frozen, staring at the two women at the end of the table. "It's not a question of marriage, exactly," she said, her eyes sidling away from Lucy's. "It's more a question of lifestyle. I don't think this is the group for you, Lucy. We've talked it over very thoroughly, and we're all in agreement. "

"And yet, you didn't see fit to inform me about this little exercise in democracy until this minute. I suppose a phone call would have been just too much effort."

"I'm sorry. We were unable to gather as a group until now." Marina swept a hand around the silent table. "But we all feel the experience you bring to the group would be too different."

"What makes it different, Marina?" The chunk of ice within Lucy exploded, sending shards of outrage everywhere. She was suffused with a blinding heat. "Do you think death comes any differently for lesbians? Do you think it feels any different to the person left behind?" She slammed the table with her open hand, making dishes clatter. The heads around the table snapped back in unison.

Lucy hardly recognized her own voice, much less the words it spewed out. "What makes it different, Marina? That little piece of paper you've got stuck in a scrapbook somewhere? That little piece of meat he had hanging between his legs?" Lucy leapt to her feet, toppling her metal chair. "Is that what makes your grief more worthy than mine?"

Marina cowered in her chair, her perfectly drawn face turned away from Lucy, both manicured hands spread palms out, as if to protect herself from a blow.

Lucy stood over her, gripping the underside of the slick white table. No one had ever been physically afraid of her before, and she realized with a sense of sick elation that it felt good. Desperately she wanted to upend the heavy table, to fling the shiny slab on its back and send china and silver crashing. It took all her strength to refrain. "You're nothing but gutless bigots," she spat out, forcing her fists down to her sides. "All of you." Lucy looked each person square in the face. "All of you." She kicked her chair away and stormed out of the house.

When she reached her car, the adrenaline deserted her, and Lucy sagged against the hood, legs trembling. Her muscles ached; each beat of her pulse jarred her entire body. She had not bothered to close the door to the house. Now, from the corner of her eye she saw a dark figure hurrying toward her out of the rectangle of light. That's all I need, thought Lucy, and pulled open her car door to escape. But the rage had left her too depleted. She sank into the driver's seat, both feet still on the curb and, fighting nausea, dropped her head into her hands.

"Professor!" called the man as he trotted down the path. "Professor!"

"Go away."

"I—look, I'm sorry. I don't agree with what went on in there."

Lucy opened one eye to see a pair of creased dress slacks and polished brown shoes. "Thank you for rising to my defense so valiantly."

"I should have. That's why I'm here." He crouched down to her eye level, and she recognized the young African-American man who had seemed vaguely familiar to her even as he had avoided her gaze in the kitchen. "Hey, are you all right?"

"I might puke, so back off."

He smiled. "You were formidable in there, but vomit doesn't scare me. I have a 3-year-old."

Lucy sat up cautiously. She looked into his square face, noting his tortoise-shell glasses, his short dreadlocks. In his toast-colored suit and forest green tie, he managed to look elegant even as he squatted in the street. "Do I know you?" she asked.

"Sort of. I work at the university."

"Oh, yes. You work in the development office."

He nodded. "I'm a fundraiser. John Harrison."

"So what are you doing out here? Marina's probably burning your membership card."

"Look, I'm sorry. Marina doesn't represent all of us. I'm ashamed that I didn't speak up in there. It *was* gutless. But I need this group." His eyes welled up.

"So do I," Lucy replied. She rose and closed her car door. In the sudden darkness they stared at one another. "What happened to your wife?"

"Asthma. About a year ago."

Lucy winced. "I'm sorry."

"What happened to yours?"

"Breast cancer, last December."

"You working yet?"

"No. Are you?"

"Yeah. I need the routine. They cut me a lot of slack at the office, though. I'm not all that productive."

Lucy glanced up at the house, where someone had by now shut the front door. "So what goes on in that group?"

"Mainly we talk, tell our stories. Talk about the stupid things people say to us. Sometimes someone brings in a book they found helpful."

"Is there a leader?"

"Well, Marina organized the group, but she doesn't dominate the discussion, believe it or not. We go around the circle, and anyone who doesn't want to talk can pass."

"So there's no curriculum? No agenda?"

"No. Just a lot of talk, and a little crying and raging."

"Does it help?"

"It helps me. I kind of live for Wednesday nights. But it might be different for you."

She bristled. "Because I'm queer?"

"Because you're a woman. I don't have anyone to talk to. All my friends are guys. And my family keeps

180

trying to marry me off." He plunged his hands into his pockets, looked at the pavement. "Brenda was everything to me."

Lucy was silent for several seconds. "Family, friends—they don't understand. That's why I thought this group . . ." Hot tears spurted to her eyes.

"Well, I was pretty hesitant about joining at first. I mean, it's like a bunch of middle-aged white people— no offense. But we've got this one thing in common, and that seems to be enough. Here." He handed her the handkerchief from his breast pocket.

"Thanks." She swiped at her cheeks. "I'm not crying. I mean, I am crying, but it's because I'm just so furious! Who the hell do they think they are? It's bad enough that I got the door slammed in my face, but it's such an insult to Claire. It's as if they're saying her life wasn't important enough, it doesn't count." Lucy blew her nose. "I forget sometimes. I forget how much we scare them."

"I know what you mean. Listen, do you want to, like, talk some time?"

She shook her head. "I don't know. Maybe."

"Well, do you want some advice?"

"Sure."

"Here's the most important thing I've figured out so far: get some new music. Don't keep listening to the songs you played with her. It's a killer. And you baby boomers need to get your heads out of the past anyway."

Lucy looked up at him, this young man with his jaunty posture and his huge burden. "Thanks. I'll keep that in mind." She handed over his handkerchief.

John took a quick step back. "No, no. That's where I draw the line. Once you blow your nose in something, it's yours."

"A good rule."

"One other thing." He jingled the change in his pockets. "The way I behaved in there? That wasn't me."

"No," said Lucy. "That wasn't me either. But I know exactly who it was."

∞ ∞ ∞ 15 ∞ ∞ ∞

SAFE AS BEANS

They stood side by side at the top of the hill, straddling their bikes. Rasheda felt like a child again. The breeze riffled across her close-cropped hair, and she wished her bicycle had long pink streamers to flap in the wind, like Keisha's.

"Ready?" she asked Lucy.

"I guess."

"And remember, the rule is to scream all the way down."

"No problem there."

"Okay. Let's go!" Rasheda gave the pedals a fierce kick. She caught her breath, uncurled her fingers from the hard rubber handlebars, and thrust her hands toward the sky. The bike raced down the hill, wobbling at first, then slicing smoothly through the air as she reminded herself to relax. Trees streaked past in a blur of gold and brown, leaves crackling under her tires. It was exhilarating: the speed, the wind, the childishness of the act, the mindless danger. "Eeyaah!" Rasheda called out, her voice trailing behind her like the absent streamers. But no voice answered her own.

Rasheda started to turn her head toward Lucy, but her bike swerved alarmingly. She coasted hands-free for another several seconds. When the road leveled off, Rasheda took control of her handlebars and glanced to the side. Lucy was rolling to a stop, fingers clutching the grips.

"I couldn't do it," Lucy confessed.

"So what? We'll try again. It was a blast."

"I don't know. It's a stupid thing to get hung up on, isn't it?"

Rasheda turned up the collar of her leather jacket. "It is possible your life could be complete even if you never get to say, 'Look Ma, no hands.'"

Lucy didn't respond. Rasheda noticed that Lucy's cheeks and the tip of her little sharp nose had turned a bright pink, two circles and a triangle so precise Keisha could have drawn them with a crayon. She glanced up at the sky, a bowl of blue above them, where a few bare branches reached toward the flat sun. Last winter, with its exhaustion and ordeals, had seemed to Rasheda like the last winter there would ever be. Yet here it was almost time for snow again.

"I just have this image in my mind," Lucy said slowly, "of Claire, on her big red bicycle with the seat perched up so high, riding down the hill in front of our house with her hands in the air."

"I thought that used to drive you crazy."

"It did." Lucy stared straight ahead at the empty intersection. "There they'd be—Claire and all the 10-year-old boys in our neighborhood, flying down the hill without holding on. Except the 10-year-olds were wearing helmets. She used to swear it was safe as beans, whatever that meant. And it looked so exciting, but I was too scared to try it. I thought it might be easier on this road, where there wouldn't be much traffic."

"No 10-year-olds, either."

"No." Lucy squeezed and released her hand brakes. "I guess I'm not cut out for hands-free flight."

"Just how safe are beans, anyway?" Rasheda pulled a pair of gloves out of her pocket. "Well, if we're not going to try again, I should head back. We're starting to make our Christmas ornaments."

"Isn't it a little early?"

"Not if you're 6."

∞ ∞ ∞

Several nights later, Rasheda pulled into her driveway and turned off the headlights. For once she did not have to steel herself for the chaos she would confront inside, because for once she had an adult babysitter. Closing the back door, she noted that the kitchen was neater than it had been when she left for work. When she looked into the living room, she found not a litter of toys and videos, but Lucy, head bent under the bamboo lamp, reading a book.

For some reason, seeing Lucy alone in her own living room made Rasheda feel a little flutter of tenderness for her. It was like that lilting moment on Keisha's birthday when Kevin marked the child's height on the kitchen doorway and they marveled at how much she'd grown—a change that seemed miraculous once they focused on it, although they had known it all along.

"How did it go?" she called out.

Lucy closed her book. "Fine. Keisha's a wonderful child, but I'm wiped out. I can't believe someone so little can run me ragged like that. I used to think teaching first-year English classes was hard."

"Their energy is incredible at this age." Rasheda crossed the hall and poked her head into Keisha's room to see her daughter sleeping amidst a herd of stuffed animals. Silently she pulled the door closed. "People say kids keep you young, but they can also make you feel old."

"You're only 35."

"And aging fast. Want a drink?"

"Sounds good."

"What'll it be?"

"Whatever you're having."

Rasheda returned with two small boxes of apple juice. "You want yours straight up or on the rocks?"

"Straight up." Lucy held the carton up to the light. "This is fascinating. I've never sipped out of a box before."

"Scary, isn't it?" She dropped onto the rounded brown couch across from Lucy's chair. "I always thought I'd be the kind of mother who made all her children's clothes and mashed home-grown vegetables for their baby food." Rasheda plunged the little straw into the carton. "Now Keisha's lucky if I turn on the stove instead of just sliding something into the microwave. And here I am drinking up her favorite juice." She took a sip. "So what did you two do tonight?"

Lucy rested her head on the back of the easy chair. "Well, let's see. We played a few hundred hands of 'Go Fish,' worked out some tunes on the piano, and then we colored for a while. By the way, Keisha left a picture for you on your pillow. It's very cute. Later I gave her a bath and tucked her into bed. Then she asked me to read to her."

"One story or three?"

"Three. How'd you know?"

"Keisha always wants either one or three. She thinks two is boring."

"Was your evening as exciting as mine?" Lucy shook her box of juice.

Rasheda kicked off her shoes and stretched out on the couch. "It was fabulous. My friend was totally surprised. Not only was she not expecting a birthday party, but it never crossed her mind that all of us maternal types could manage a girls' night out."

"Why? I thought all your friends were married."

"Not all husbands can manage kids on their own, you know. Kevin's pretty exceptional. He was even willing to give up his poker night if we couldn't find child care. Thank goodness you volunteered, because I would have owed him big time."

"What would he have made you do?"

"Oh, I don't know. Sew on a button. Cook some okra. Something horrible." Rasheda laced her fingers behind her head. "It was so much fun tonight, getting together with my girlfriends. I miss that. When I lived in Washington, I used to spend a lot of time hanging out with my sisters and our women friends. We used to have slumber parties, go away for weekends together. We'd stay up all night playing cards and laughing—and this was after we were all grown up, and old enough to pay for it the next day."

"How come you don't do that any more?"

"I'm much busier now, and so are the friends I've made up here. Seems like we're all running as fast as we can just to stay in place, with kids and work and responsibilities." It occurred to Rasheda that many elements of her life had fallen away. Each day now seemed to be about gathering strength for the next.

"What about your women's group at church?"

"I had to drop that last year."

"When Claire got sick?"

Rasheda nodded, sucking on the tiny straw.

"Rasheda, I've been thinking . . ." Lucy turned her empty carton around and around in her hands. "Maybe it would be fun to take this 'aunt' thing more seriously. A lot of the time now, I don't feel entirely . . . here. But when I'm with Keisha, it's different. You *have* to be engaged when Keisha's around. I mean, tonight she was playing Claire's piano, and her little head was bobbing, and her eyes were so sparkly. Watching her made me feel, I don't know, alive, and grateful to be alive. So I was wondering if we could make this a regular event."

"Like what?"

"Well, maybe I could babysit once a week or something."

Rasheda laughed. "Girl, you don't know what you're getting yourself into. Let's start with every couple of weeks. How about every other Friday? That would coincide with Kevin's poker night." She clasped her hands together. "That would mean I could see my girlfriends, or take myself to a lecture on campus, or just go shopping if I wanted. Anything I wanted."

"So it's okay?"

"I'd love it. A little speck of freedom twice a month. And I won't even have to worry about what the babysitter's letting her watch on TV."

"Nothing but nature shows, I promise."

"Some of those are the goriest stories around."

"Those are the ones we'll be watching."

"Oh, great, then I'll have to deal with her nightmares. That reminds me." Rasheda hurried into the bedroom and returned with a towering basket of clean laundry. "The nightmare of the never-ending chore." She dumped it onto the couch.

"I'll help you," offered Lucy.

"Here." She transferred an armful of colorful clothes onto Lucy's ottoman. "You can do Keisha's things. I don't think you can deal with Kevin's boxers."

"Right again." Lucy held up a tiny turtleneck. "Look at this. These are like little doll clothes."

"If dolls spilled mustard on their shirts." Hands moving swiftly, Rasheda smoothed a white t-shirt against the brown couch and folded it into a tidy packet. "Lucy, did I tell you they finally hired Mark to take Claire's job?"

"I thought no one was very impressed with him."

"Well, I'm not. Turns out my opinion doesn't carry much weight in the executive offices."

Lucy rolled up a pair of yellow socks. "What's wrong with Mark, anyway?"

"He's like a walking emergency. You know, Claire used to turn work into an adventure. Not that she didn't take it seriously—girlfriend had a work ethic that didn't stop. But there was joy in it, and discovery too." Rasheda paused, but her hands continued their smooth labor. "Claire always wanted to try something new. Even when we were under a lot of pressure, she'd take the time to show me things. She was always saying, 'Now, watch how I do this so you can do it next time.'" Rasheda chuckled. "Whenever we'd finish editing a news clip or something right before air time, she'd make this little cartoonish sound. '*Squeeek!*'"

"You mean like a mouse?"

"No, like squeaking in just before the deadline."

Lucy smiled. "I didn't know that."

"Now Mark, he's a different story. Everything's a crisis to him. We can be editing some dinky station ID, and he'll be cracking his knuckles the whole time."

"Yuck."

"I know. His favorite phrases are, 'We don't have time for that,' and 'Let's do it quick and dirty.'"

"So why did Gerald hire him?"

"Mark's been 'acting senior editor' for months. I guess Gerald finally accepted the fact that he's the best they're going to find in this market."

"I'm sorry." Lucy did not look up from her folding. "That must have been especially disappointing for you."

"For me? Why?"

"Well, you were interested in that job, weren't you?"

Rasheda shot her a sharp glance. "Lucy, I never wanted Claire's job. I don't have anywhere near the experience."

"Then I don't understand."

"What don't you understand?"

"Why you worked so hard after Claire got sick. She missed you, you know. She wanted to spend more time with you, but you were too busy working."

"I was trying to save Claire's job." Rasheda felt her heart begin to press against her chest. "I didn't want to give them an excuse to replace her."

"What difference would that have made? You knew she wasn't coming back. Harry says it was for the insurance, but that can't be right."

Rasheda shook out a bright red shirt. "Of course that's right. There's no way you could have paid for Claire's treatment on one salary."

"But you can keep your insurance for 18 months. Connie Walker said Claire couldn't survive anywhere near that long."

Rasheda remembered seeing Dr. Walker at the funeral: a tall gaunt woman, one of maybe half a dozen brown faces in a sea of white. She remembered exchanging glances with her during the service.

Afterward, Rasheda had stared when Dr. Walker flung herself into Lucy's arms, sobbing as if Claire had been the only patient she had ever lost. Rasheda had clenched Kevin's sleeve and turned away. Her friends had put their fate in the hands of this woman, and she had answered their faith with a timetable. It astonished her still that Claire—rebellious, defiant Claire—had followed that edict practically to the day. It had been Claire's last deadline.

"Connie Walker isn't God, Lucy! She's just a doctor. She didn't know. What if Claire had lived longer? What if she had outlived her insurance?"

"Oh, Rasheda." Lucy clutched one of Keisha's shirts to her own chest. "You gave up your last few hours with Claire for that?"

Tears prickled at the back of Rasheda's throat. "Yes, for that! I neglected my daughter. I fought with my husband. I stared at those monitors until I was seeing double—all for Claire, and for you, just in case she could pull through a little longer." It had been ridiculous, Rasheda saw now, a prayer offered to the wind, to think her sacrifice could magically save Claire. She slapped a stack of t-shirts into the basket. "And all this time you thought I was after her job?"

"Well, yes. I didn't know what else to think. I mean, I'll always be grateful for everything you did for us. But at the same time I was angry at you for the hours you couldn't be there. I know it's not rational. Or fair."

"Well, why didn't you tell me then? Why didn't you ask me what was going on?"

"I tried."

"When?"

"I don't remember. But I remember trying."

"So now it's been, what—a year that you've held on to this? You let something simmer for that long, and someone's bound to get burned."

"I'm sorry, Rasheda."

"You should be." Rasheda pushed past Lucy's chair and hurried down the basement stairs to the joyless corner where the washer and dryer huddled under a tangle of pipes. Kevin had been promising to paint this area for ages, but time for such extras was hard to find. And now Rasheda discovered that all those hours of overtime she had eked out had been not only useless, but resented.

She jerked open the dryer door and began to yank sheets and towels into the plastic basket. But how could

Lucy have known what she was up to? They had never discussed insurance or finances or any of the practicalities except how to keep Claire comfortable. Even that they had not been able to manage.

Claire would have howled if she had guessed the reason for Rasheda's sudden compulsion to juggle both their jobs. "You're only fooling yourself," she would have said. "You don't have the power to keep me alive." And of course Rasheda didn't—just as she hadn't had the power to keep her mother alive, no matter how much she bargained with God.

Rasheda closed the dryer door and leaned against it. Her frantic work had been just an offering, childish and futile, to distract her from the truth she had always known. She was not in control. She could not even make safe the small world that surrounded her daughter. Anyone could be taken from Rasheda at any moment.

She remembered how she had felt last weekend, soaring hands-free on her bike, freedom flowing through her fingers. Probably it all had to do with physics, but Rasheda had sensed it was the hand of God keeping her upright. Faith, she knew, was the opposite of fear. It was a lesson she daily struggled to remember.

"Rasheda, I'm really sorry," blurted Lucy as Rasheda emerged into the living room. "I feel like the one good thing to come out of all of this is that you and I are truly friends now, not just through Claire. I hope I haven't messed that up."

"You are working my last nerve, but it hasn't snapped yet." Rasheda shoved the new basket of laundry toward her. "Here's your punishment. More mindless labor."

"Does this mean we're okay?" Lucy asked.

"We're cool."

She exhaled loudly. "Good. I'd hate to be at odds with you. Claire told me you were tough to rile, but once you were mad—watch out." Lucy rose to fold the bath towels against the length of her body. "Should I tell you a secret?"

"Okay." Rasheda took a last sip of apple juice.

"I love mindless labor."

"Is that why you stayed in school all those years?"

"That's probably why I love it so much. You know how I've been looking around for some other kind of work?"

"Yes."

"Well, I got a job. Claire and I have this friend who's a caterer, and right before Thanksgiving I'm going to start working in her kitchen."

"You're going to be a chef?"

"Not a chef, just a helper. You know, chopping vegetables, cleaning produce, that kind of thing."

Rasheda tossed a roll of socks into the basket. "Cleaning and chopping? That's your plan?"

"If I had a plan, I wouldn't be me."

"You know, the women in my family broke their butts to avoid working in someone else's kitchen. And you, with your education, that's what you want to do?"

"For a while."

Rasheda shook her head. "What about the university?"

"I'm on unpaid leave for a year. After that, I don't know."

Rasheda finished folding and slid her basket next to the coffee table. "I don't get it. Why would you want this job? You know it won't pay squat."

"But it'll keep me moving. Besides, at the end of my work day, there will be beautiful food and a clean kitchen. What could be better than that?"

"So this is an interim thing, not a permanent career move."

"Probably. Who knows?"

They were silent for a few moments as Lucy tucked the last sheet into her basket. "What do you suppose Claire would think about this?" mused Rasheda.

"I wish I could ask her. Not that you'd necessarily have to ask in order to hear Claire's opinion."

"You mean she'd tell you, 'do this' or 'don't do that'?"

"No. She wouldn't tell me anything. She'd ask me questions."

"Oh, yes. I know those questions."

Lucy stretched back in her chair, swung her feet up on the ottoman. "I remember this one time, years and years ago. I had been fighting with my brother Alex. We hadn't spoken for a month."

"What was the fight about?"

She squinted at the ceiling. "Do you know, I can't recall? But I remember Claire pressing me about it. 'What do you see happening now, Lucy?' she used to ask me. 'Do you intend never to talk to him again? For how long—until one of your parents dies? Will you ignore Alex at the funeral? He's your only sibling. Do you expect to grow some new ones?' Eventually I called him, and we patched it up. Not because Claire encouraged me to. Because she made me think about the future." Lucy sighed. "But I don't want to think about the future right now. That's why I want to chop vegetables."

"Can't say I can picture you in that job." Rasheda gazed around, at the landscape of folded laundry, at the kitchen doorway through which Kevin would stride any minute, at the island of ivory light in which Lucy reclined. "But I guess if it doesn't interfere with your babysitting duties, it's okay with me."

∞ ∞ ∞ 15 ∞ ∞ ∞

THE INVITATION

Jane loved spending the night at Roxanne's house, a sweet little cottage composed of kitchen, living room, and study clustered beneath a sloping roof. "It looks like you!" she had exclaimed when Roxanne first invited her over.

"It looks like the home of someone who's spent the last decade paying off school loans," Roxanne had replied.

Both were true. The spartan house did resemble Roxanne—organized, efficient, but whimsical. Jane loved the nightly ritual of transforming the living room into a bedroom. The two women unfolded the futon, smoothed out the bedding and clicked off the lamp, turning toward one another in the faint glow from the phosphorescent galaxy Roxanne had painted on the ceiling. For years Jane had wished she had stars on her own ceiling, but she had never acted on the urge. So she had been both thrilled and impressed to discover stars glittering in the dark of Roxanne's tiny house. Now, months after that discovery, Jane's pleasure was dulled only by her girlfriend's annoying habit of needing to sleep.

"Roxanne, I know I said I'd be quiet now, but did I tell you about the intense faculty meeting this afternoon? I thought Ralph and Mary Ann were going to start punching each other. She is so inflexible."

"Okay, that does it." Roxanne rolled onto her side and pressed her palm against Jane's lips. "I am a desperate woman. I've tried begging, I've tried pleading, I've tried ignoring you. Now I'll try bribery." She reached across Jane for the pewter bowl that held her pocket change. "Jane, I will pay you to shut up. I will pay you one nickel for every minute you stay silent."

"I can't help it." Jane blocked her arm. "I babble when I'm happy."

"I know," murmured Roxanne, "and I'm glad you're so happy. But I can't stay awake another second."

"Okay, but let me tell you one more thing."

"Are you going to torture your friends like this in that cabin next weekend?"

"We have separate rooms. Do you want to hear about this meeting or not?"

"Not."

"A mortal conflict is ripping apart the department that employs the woman you love, and you don't want to know about it?" Jane waited for a response. "Not even a little?" But it was no use. Roxanne was gone.

With a sigh, Jane sat up on one elbow. At 45 years of age, romance had ambushed her and smacked her silly. No longer did she crave long nights of solitude with her books and music; no longer did she need to eat or sleep. Instead, she was filled with a giddy energy that hurtled her through the daylight hours and ignited each evening into passion.

She had been shocked to discover that middle-aged love felt no less intoxicating than the teen-aged variety. Granted, Jane knew better now than to blab about her beloved all day long, but she wished she could. Her students, she was sure, must have noticed a new animation in her hands as they sent words winging through the air. And her friends seemed pleased for her, teasing her only gently about this late-in-life conversion to the joys of coupledom.

Best of all, Roxanne seemed no less besotted—only more tired. In the fading illumination from the overhead stars, Jane smiled down at her. Roxanne was the perfect sleeper, with her soft silvery hair, her sweet closed eyes fringed in long spiky lashes. Awake, she was like an impressionist painting: all motion and light, quick precise movements and sparkling energy. In slumber, Roxanne was so still that Jane could barely tell they shared a bed unless they were actually touching.

With a yawn, Jane lowered her head to the pillow and slowed her breathing to fall into rhythm with Roxanne's. Maybe she could trick sleep into visiting her as well.

Hours later, Jane awakened into a dense, featureless darkness. It was so peaceful here in Roxanne's cottage; Jane heard none of the sounds that punctuated her nighttimes at home—no dogs barking, no furnace roaring to life. With a surge of terror, Jane realized she could hear nothing at all.

She tried to speak, but her throat had seized up. Desperately she wanted to wake Roxanne, asleep just inches away, but Jane's body had turned to stone. She struggled to move, to cough, to click her teeth together—anything to make a sound. The silence pressed in, paralyzing her. Finally she managed to thrash one numb arm against the night table, knocking off the pewter bowl.

The bowl crashed to the ground. Coins rained down, rolling across the wooden floor and rocking to a halt with the racket of snare drums. It made a gorgeous din.

Roxanne shot out of bed. "What's wrong?"

"I just spilled your bowl of coins. I'm sorry."

"God. I thought the roof had fallen in or something." Roxanne let herself be tugged back under the covers.

"I know, but everything's fine."

"Then why do you look so upset?"

Jane swiped at her eyes. "I'm not upset. I'm just—relieved. I woke up and it was so quiet, I thought I had gone deaf."

"Oh, honey." Roxanne cupped her palm against Jane's cheek. "That could never happen. It won't descend on you suddenly."

"Why not? It descended on my father suddenly."

"No it didn't. It couldn't have. You were a child. Probably they didn't tell you about it until his condition was quite advanced."

"I suppose so." Jane ducked her head. "I feel so stupid. But it was scary, that heavy silence. I was in a panic. Roxanne, if we're going to stay together, you might need to move somewhere noisier."

"Maybe I could learn to snore."

Jane pulled the comforter up to her shoulders. "You know, you were like a little pajama warrior, leaping to the rescue. I was very impressed."

"Glad I could entertain you. Now how about getting some Z's?"

"I'll try."

"Try hard, okay?"

As a watery light threaded its way under the window shade, Jane closed her eyes and sank into sleep, giving her fate one more day to find her.

∞ ∞ ∞

Rasheda had been running late since she first opened her eyes. It was not yet 7, and already she had showered, awakened her husband, and settled sleepy-eyed Keisha in front of a bowl of hot cereal and a picture book. Now she was in the bedroom ironing a blouse for work, the phone tucked precariously between ear and shoulder.

"It sounds like fun, Lucy, but I can't do it."

"Why not?"

"I can't just take off and go like you non-mom types." Rasheda nosed the iron around the flat, squarish mother-of-pearl buttons. "I have a helpless little creature at home. Two, if you count Keisha."

"Very funny!" called Kevin from the steamy bathroom.

"But that's the beauty of it," Lucy enthused, her voice skittery and thin in Rasheda's ear. "It's only one night. We drive up there Friday after work, eat a gluttonous dinner, light a fire, and talk till we drop. The next day we hike, snack, and get home before dark. It'll be like a mini-vacation for you—the last escape before winter sets in."

Rasheda unplugged the iron. "I don't know. Who's making this sinful meal?"

"Jane's making her famous farm dinner."

"With the baked chicken and homemade noodles?"

"That's the one. And I'm bringing a chocolate mousse cake that's so rich I'll have to slice it with a scalpel."

"Ooh, Lucy, you temptress."

"Harry's in charge of drinks and he's already signed up for dish duty. By the way, I had to rent the cabin for the entire weekend, so if Kevin and Keisha wanted to meet you up there on Saturday night, you could have the whole place to yourselves. Check-out's not until 2 on Sunday."

"Let me get this straight. My only responsibility is to eat, drink, and be beautiful, plus my family gets to stay up there the second night for free." Rasheda stepped into her slacks.

"Right."

"So how'd I get to be queen for a day?"

"I figured it was the only way to entice you."

"Well, consider me enticed. I'll talk it over with Kevin, but you know it's a long shot."

"I know. It's just that, well, I've been kind of despondent lately, and having all my friends around might pick up my spirits."

"Now, how am I supposed to say no to that? Girl, that is so low!"

"What's up?" asked Kevin a few minutes later as he leaned into the mirror to arrange his tie.

"Lucy's rented a cabin in Monroe for the weekend, and she wants me to go up there with her and the others Friday night. They're all clearing out on Saturday afternoon, so we could have the cabin for the rest of the weekend, on Lucy's tab."

"Mama, I'm done," called Keisha from the kitchen.

"Okay, honey, now what do you do next?"

"What? I forget."

"Put your bowl in the sink and go get dressed. I laid your clothes out on the bed."

"Will you come help me?"

Kevin replied, "I'll help you, sweetheart. Be right there."

"What do you think?" Rasheda asked. "Could you handle Keisha overnight?"

He pulled on his suit jacket. "Despite what you tell your friends, I'm not helpless. I'll take her to my mother's."

Rasheda gave him a pat on the rear. "That's my man."

A half hour later, after waving Keisha onto the school bus, the Coopers sat in their car, enjoying a moment of stillness while the engine warmed.

"Do you want me to pick up one of those tests after work today?" offered Kevin.

"You'd pick up a pregnancy test, but you won't buy tampons?"

"It's different."

She smiled. "I know. I'll run out at lunch and get one. There's a brand I like."

"Okay, but don't take the test at work. I want us to find out together."

"All right." Briefly, she leaned her head on his shoulder. "Let's not talk about it any more. It's bad luck."

"You know, it might do you good to have a girls' night out." Kevin twisted the knob on the finicky radio. "Although I don't know why you can't have one right here in town with your own friends."

"What do you mean, my own friends?"

"Rasheda, I know you were close to Claire, but there aren't many of *us* in her crowd, are there?"

"Not many of *them* in our crowd, either. Besides, our crowd all has kids, and their husbands aren't half as capable as you."

"Now you're trying to butter me up."

"That's true. But you know, it's not a girls' night out. Harry will be there too." She flicked on the heater.

"I can't decide if the man is incredibly brave or a total fool. Anyway, you do need a vacation." He eased the car into gear. "Come to think of it, so do I. Maybe we could both stay home today and heat up the house a little bit. What do you say?"

Rasheda snapped her seat belt into place. "I'd love it. But they might notice if you don't go to school. You're the teacher."

∞ ∞ ∞

"I wish you could go with me tomorrow night," Harry murmured. Eyes closed, he lay on his side on the black leather couch in his own living room, his head resting in Martha's lap. He could feel the little ridges of her corduroy pants against his cheek. "Why can't you?"

"Let me count the ways," she replied in her husky, thrilling voice. It was a voice that suggested smooth whiskey and wild companions, late nights and danger- ous choices. It was a voice that had almost nothing in common with the strong, steady, generous woman Harry was learning to know, and the contrast delighted him.

"Have I been invited?" asked Martha, combing her fingers through his hair.

"No."

"Have I met any of the other people?"

"No."

"Do they even know about me?"

"Not yet."

"Sounds perfect. I'll go pack."

"But you would fit in perfectly," he insisted.

"Why? Because I'm not a teenager like all your other conquests?"

"Well, yeah. But also because they would like you. You'd have things to talk about. And Claire would have loved you." Harry tucked his finger between the middle two buttons of her blouse. Martha's flesh was soft and giving, a sensuous contrast to the rock-hard torsos of the women he was used to. But he could never tell Martha this; fit and athletic as she was, she might take it the wrong way. By the same token, Harry struggled to find a way to explain to her what an ongoing revelation it was to discover the complex, compelling sexuality of a woman his own age. He wished he could talk to Claire about it. She would help him find the words.

"Why would she have loved me?"

"Because you don't let me get away with anything, and neither did she." He slid open one of the buttons. "I can just picture the four of us hanging out together—you and me, Claire and Lucy. You know, a double date."

"A double date. I haven't heard that expression since the eighth grade. Would you buy me a milk-shake?"

"Sure. Fries, too."

"Harry, do you ever think that by getting involved with me, at some level deep inside you might be trying to win Claire's approval?"

He opened another button. "I'm not trying to win anyone's approval. I'm trying to get you to take your clothes off."

"Forget it. I'm leaving early tonight, remember? So we can both get to work on time for a change?"

Harry liked to imagine Martha's bustling, red-faced arrivals at the Sterling *Daily News*, the amused expressions of her colleagues, already at their desks in the newsroom. "Oh, all right." He hauled himself to a sitting position. From there he had a better view of Martha's thick chestnut hair, her brown eyes and deli-cate chin, the smiling parentheses that bordered her full lips.

"So what will you be doing," she asked, "alone there in the wilderness with three women?"

"Just visiting, I guess. Although Lucy seemed to have something in mind when she invited me. But don't worry, my virtue will be perfectly safe."

"Your virtue is something I never worry about."

"I've never had that, you know." Harry rubbed his hand across his square, scratchy jaw.

"What, virtue?"

"No, a double date. I mean, I've always had my friendship with Claire"—with palms parallel to one another, he described a chopping motion in the air, as if setting down a heavy stack of books directly to his left—"and my romantic life." Harry made the same motion to his right. "There's never been any way to connect the two. Maybe I've never been with the kind of woman who could bridge the gap. And now that I am, it's too late."

"Too late for me to get to know Claire, maybe, but not too late for you to connect all the parts of your life. What about Lucy?"

"You'll meet Lucy, and maybe you'll become friends. But compared to Claire, even Lucy is a new friend."

"I want to meet your friends, Harry, and your siblings, and—who knows?—maybe even your parents some day. But for now," she squeezed his knee, "I should head for home."

"Stay with me," he murmured, his lips moving against her smooth, sensitive ear.

"Harry . . ."

"We'll get up early. I'll make you breakfast. We'll get to work in plenty of time. Just stay."

"All right, I'll stay," Martha agreed in her midnight voice.

His mouth still pressed against the side of her face, Harry smiled.

∞ ∞ ∞ **17** ∞ ∞ ∞

LIVING IN THE FIRST PERSON

"Never again in life," groaned Rasheda. She hung her arms over the sides of the padded rocking chair and let her head loll against the back.

"Never again what?" asked Lucy, stretched out on the nubby, rust-colored couch.

"Never again will I consume so many quality calories in one sitting," she vowed.

Squatting in front of the stone fireplace, Jane broke a piece of kindling across her knee. "We dined at the kitchen table and moved out here for dessert. Technically, that's two sittings."

"Oh, good. I feel much better."

"Do you feel good enough to waddle over here and give me a hand?"

"I'm not sure. Would that involve moving?"

"I'll help." Lucy jumped off the couch. "I only had one slice of cake." She reached for the poker and pried up a heavy log so Jane could wedge pieces of kindling beneath it.

"That cake was fantastic," Harry called from the kitchen, raising his voice above the running water. "Where'd you get it, Lucy?"

"I didn't buy it. I made it."

"You baked and frosted all those thin little layers of cake?"

"Amazing the things you have time for when you don't have a job." Lucy returned the poker to its metal stand.

"I'm finished!" Harry announced. "That didn't take too long." He strode into the living room, wiping his hands on his jeans, and settled on the oval rag rug in front of the couch. His long legs stretched across the floor, almost reaching the runners of Rasheda's chair.

Lucy stepped over him on her way back to the couch. She noted his worn hiking boots, faded jeans, and plaid flannel shirt, his thick sandy hair brushed back from his square forehead. "Harry, you look like you belong here. All you need is a beard and you'd look perfectly at home."

"Good food, a healthy fire, and three beautiful women. Why shouldn't I look content?"

Eyes closed, fingers laced across her belly, Rasheda snorted. "Please do not practice your skills on us."

"Besides, beards are for guys with weak chins," he pointed out.

"No, you definitely have a smug look about you tonight." Her cheeks pink from the fire, Jane curled up in the large battered easy chair that faced the couch. "What is it you're not telling us?"

"Are you some kind of detective?"

"You're not exactly subtle. Who is she?"

He grinned. "Her name's Martha. I met her at the dentist's office."

"The hygienist?" guessed Rasheda.

"No, just a patient."

"I didn't know you saw a pediatric dentist," said Jane.

"Very funny. Martha's different from all the others. For one thing, she's my age."

"What possessed you?" Rasheda asked.

Lucy watched the tender skin on the back of Harry's neck redden as he answered. "I just wanted someone I could talk to. Guess that means I'm getting old."

"You mean you never wanted that before?" Jane stared at him.

"Well, no. It never really occurred to me before. I don't know why not."

"You had Claire," Rasheda pointed out.

"What's that got to do with it?"

"Claire was the woman in your life," she explained. "That left you free to pursue girls."

"Tell us more about her," urged Jane.

"Martha's a reporter for the *News*. She's smart, funny and . . . gorgeous."

"Oh, my God." Jane pressed her hand to her heart. "Not cute? Not a babe? No resemblance to Barbie whatsoever?"

"Nope. And sexy as hell."

"But you told me you'd given up on love." Lucy was embarrassed by the plaintive tone in her own voice. "You told me relationships were too hard, and you were going to live your life alone."

"Hey, it's been over 2 months. That was a long time for me."

"You think 2 months is a long time to be alone?" Jane interjected. "Try it for 3 years."

"What is this," demanded Rasheda, "the celibacy Olympics?"

"Guess I'll be going for the gold," said Lucy.

Harry swivelled to look up at her. "Do you ever think about . . . ?"

"Sex?"

"No, I meant going out again. You know, dating, or whatever we should call it now that we're ancient."

"God, no. The idea's just . . ." Lucy shuddered.

"I know it sounds impossible to you now," Rasheda ventured, "but people do recover in time. Some even remarry. I know you're not there yet, but someday you might think about it."

Jane leaned toward Lucy, elbows on her knees. "In fact, Roxanne has a couple of friends she thinks you might like. I'm not talking about romance here, just getting to know some new people."

Speechless, Lucy stared at the fire. Until this moment she had felt extraordinarily light here in this wooden cabin where she had never been with Claire. The small world wrapped around her, snug and varnished as a ship: the windowless kitchen, the square living room with its arched stone fireplace, the four discreet doors leading to bedrooms and bath. Outside, she knew, the forest swept up into mountain peaks poking the glittery sky. But none of it was visible in the overcast night.

As the silence lengthened, Lucy grew intensely aware of the rhythmic creak of Rasheda's rocker, the *skritch* of barren branches against the thin windows. The weight of her solitude came crushing down. She saw she would never narrow the distance between herself and everyone on earth who had not been bereaved. Because here she was with her closest friends, and they wanted her to start dating. Dating! With what—this weary body? This ruined heart? Who could bear to touch her, to feel the river of grief running beneath her skin? With whom could Lucy ever share the new, harrowing way she had learned to love?

Lucy struggled to her feet and dropped another log on the fire. "Let's talk about something else. In fact, let's play a game."

"I've got a couple in my bag," Rasheda offered.

"I was thinking of a game you didn't bring. Something along the lines of Clue."

"You mean as in, 'Colonel Mustard in the library with a pistol'?" asked Harry.

"No, more like 'Ms. Morganstern in the Midwest with a checkbook.'"

"Oh, Lucy!" Jane dropped her forehead into her hands. "I can't believe you dragged us up here to badger us about that property in Wisconsin. I thought you were determined to leave Claire her secrets."

Lucy turned to face them, the fire roasting her hands as she clenched them behind her back. "I am. I'm not going to pursue the land—I'm not going to see it, not going to research it. In fact, the property's already on the market. Turns out the deed was in my study the whole time, one of the millions of papers I had to sign."

"Then what's the problem?" asked Harry.

"I just need to remember what was going on in her life when she bought the property. Maybe it is ridiculous, but I can't let it rest. Five years ago, why would Claire have been in Wisconsin? Did she go on a business trip? Did she have some kind of family event? You have to help me think." She paced the stone hearth.

"Look, Lucy, I still lived in Washington then, so I don't have a clue what Claire was up to." Rasheda brought her rocker to a stop. "But I'll tell you this: you're making a big mistake to keep driving yourself crazy over this. You may never know what was on that girl's mind, but you know for sure she wasn't trying to run away from you."

"How can I know that, when I can't even figure out what the hell she was doing in the Midwest?"

"You took her there," blurted Jane.

"Me?"

"Yes. I just remembered. You took her to Chicago with you for an academic conference."

"You're right. It was the MLA!" exclaimed Lucy. "The Modern Language Association conference was in Chicago, and we flew there together to do some sight-seeing before it started."

They had visited the Art Institute, the Field Museum, the Sears Tower. They had overdosed on ribs, crunched across the frigid sand of the lakefront, stayed up late to hear blues in crowded clubs. Then Lucy went to attend her conference, and Claire had flown on to—where?

"She told me she was going to Duluth," mused Lucy.

"Duluth isn't too far from that area of Wisconsin," said Jane. "Why was she going there?"

"To visit her Aunt Stella—who, as it turns out, is not related to Claire at all."

Rasheda interrupted. "Now, before you get all paranoid about this, let me remind you that I have a daughter who calls you Aunt Lucy, and you don't resemble a soul in our family."

"Keisha's 6 years old!"

"What do you think she's going to call you when she's 40—Dr. Rogers? Come on, Lucy. You've had your attitude in the upright and locked position since you first heard about this stupid property. It's time to let it go."

"That's so easy for you to say, Rasheda." Lucy ran her hands through her hair, making it crackle with static electricity. "You don't know what it's like. You think all the letting go is over when someone dies? That's when it's just beginning.

"Look, you're all telling me to drop the subject. But the subject isn't some little patch of land somewhere. I don't give a damn about that. The subject is whether or not I knew my lover."

"Of course you knew Claire," cried Jane. "We all did. That's how I know there's no way she was hiding some kind of secret life."

"You can't live a secret life on 1.5 acres of unimproved land," Harry pointed out.

"Then why didn't Claire tell me about it?"

"We don't know," Rasheda said quietly. "We're not going to know. And it's going to hurt you, but you already knew about some serious blues before this property thing came along."

"That's true." Lucy glanced at her red scorched hands. "I did." She stepped across Harry's legs and dropped onto the couch.

"So now we're going to play a different game," announced Rasheda.

"Thank God," breathed Harry. "What's it called?"

"It's called 'Name That Tune.' And the tune is Claire."

"Wait for me!" Jane called from the kitchen. She hurried out with four glasses and a bottle of wine. "Did you say 'Name That Tune'?"

Rasheda nodded. "We're going to lay to rest the notion that there was something furtive about Claire's life. And we're going to do it by telling stories that name her."

"Name her?" Lucy watched Jane pull out the cork, twist by squeaky twist.

"Stories that remind us of who she was. Harry, would you pump up the fire? I'll start." Holding her empty glass between two fingers, Rasheda stared into the rectangular space between their chairs. Finally she began.

"Gerald, our boss, is a basketball nut. He loves that game more than anything in the world. One day he and some of the other guys at the station were talking about a women's college game. I guess the station had televised it the previous night. Anyway, they were all talking about it, and they were laughing."

"Because all the coaches are lesbians?" asked Jane, proffering the bottle.

"Are they?" Rasheda covered her glass with her hand.

"Maybe not all. But a lot."

"Well, that's not what these guys were laughing at. They were just doing their usual macho jive about how women athletes couldn't hope to compete with men. So Claire said, in her sweetest voice, that she's pretty sure a lot of women could beat Gerald at basketball." Rasheda was smiling now, her eyes still focused on the middle distance.

"Gerald said 'Oh, yeah? Like who?' 'Like me,' she answered. Then he fell out laughing. After he got control of himself he asked, 'Would you like to put a little wager on that? You and me going one on one.'

"'Why not?' Claire replied. All this time, she's perfectly relaxed, with a pleasant little expression on her face.

"'I could sure use the cash,' Gerald told her, and now he's snickering. 'How much do you want to place on this little bet?'

"Without changing her demeanor at all, Claire says slowly, 'One thousand dollars.'"

Rasheda took a moment to giggle. "Lucy, you know how ruddy Gerald's complexion is. Well, he turned dead white. 'You must be good if you're willing to put up that kind of money,' he says. 'I am,' Claire nods. 'I'm damned good.' He swallows hard. 'Well, how come you never told me before?' Claire just smiled up at him. 'You never asked.'"

"So did he withdraw from the bet?" asked Lucy.

"In a flash. Later, after Gerald had left the edit suite, I asked her if she was really such a great player. 'I haven't picked up a basketball since high school,' she told me. 'But these boys need to be taken down a peg every now and then.'"

"I don't think that story is all that funny," Harry declared.

"Then you tell us one." Lucy patted the couch beside her.

Harry unfolded himself from the floor to join her. He flung one leg over the arm of the couch, stretched the other in front of Lucy's feet. "Claire and I used to go on these expeditions to find exotic food. I remember this one night we were at a Thai restaurant in Ithaca. It wasn't even a restaurant, just a private house where once a month the family opened up a big back room and cooked dinner for the public. I don't know how Claire found out about it.

"She ordered this squid dish, which was listed on the menu with five stars—the hottest. The owner took our order, and he kept saying to Claire, 'Oh no, Mrs. Five star. Native Thai only. Too hot for you, Mrs.' But of course she insisted.

"So they brought our order. Claire took a couple of bites, and damn if she didn't turn bright red. Tears streamed down her face. She had to eat two bowls of that sweet coconut ice cream to calm down her taste buds."

"Didn't that make her sick?" asked Rasheda.

"Hell, no. She proceeded to eat half my dinner. When the owner came over with the check, Claire told him, 'You were absolutely right. Five stars was way too hot for me. I should have listened to you.' And he smiled and said, 'Oh no, Mrs. That was four stars.'

"She stared at him. 'You told the kitchen four stars, even though I ordered five?' He nodded. 'Yes, Mrs. I deceived you.' Well, I thought his life was over. But instead Claire broke into this big grin and said,

'Hey, thanks! I owe you one.' So from then on, whenever Claire was bull-headed about something, I would tell her, 'Oh no, Mrs.'"

"Did it stop her?" asked Rasheda.

"Of course not. But it made me feel better, to remember a time she had been humbled by a spice."

"I have a story to tell," announced Jane. "Lucy, you already know this one."

As Jane related the story of Claire forcing her to confront her hearing loss, Lucy found her mind wandering. It was so like Claire to hold on to her touching faith in technology: she had no doubt that a test could assess Jane's condition, a treatment could cure it. And yet, technology had failed Claire utterly. No matter where she looked, Lucy kept bouncing against the hard, accidental fact of it. Forget the mammograms, the clinical exams, the sonograms. Lucy had found the killer herself, with her bare hands, in an act of passion.

"It feels better now that I've told you," Jane concluded. She scooted back in the large chair and pulled her knees up to her chest. "That's one thing about Claire that always impressed me. She could keep a secret. Not just secrets, but . . . she held all my stories for me."

"What do you mean?" asked Rasheda.

"Every drama I've ever had, every new love, every heartache, every fresh job, every big idea about what to do with my life—I've always shared them with Claire. Now I don't know what to do with all my stories. It's like learning to live in the first person."

"Why don't you tell Roxanne?" Lucy suggested.

"I guess I could from now on, but Roxanne is a case in point. Here's someone who has grown so important to me, and yet she's never met Claire. She'll never know my father. I can tell her anecdotes and show her pictures, but it's still as if she opened the book in the middle."

They fell silent, letting the fire carry the conversation. Lucy stared down at the inverted reflection inside her wine glass. She realized that the four of them were no longer playing a game but creating a work of art: the portrait of a missing person, etched in absence. Each of them would always recognize the particular details and dimensions of the space Claire left behind.

"I remember a time," Lucy began slowly. "It was close to the end, right around this time of year, I think. Claire hadn't been eating much, but she developed this craving for strawberries." She turned to Harry. "Remember? I asked you to find some, and you had to scout all over town."

He nodded. "They were out of season. All I could find was cranberries."

Lucy faced the women again. "Finally he managed to get a couple of pints, and I washed some and put them in a bowl for her. She chewed each one so slowly. I asked her why she had this sudden attraction for strawberries.

"'Strawberries are like me,' she said.

"'What do you mean?' I asked.

"'No one expects them to last forever.'"

Jane blew out a sharp puff of air. "On that note, " she said, gulping back her own glass of wine. "I propose a new game."

"Oh, man," groaned Harry. "Couldn't we just watch TV or something?"

"It's called Truth," continued Jane.

"Truth or Dare?" he asked. "Truth or Consequences?"

"No, just Truth."

He buried his face in his long hands. "That's what I was afraid of."

"The truth is, we have to stop meeting like this." Jane's voice was strained and dry.

"Is that a joke?" asked Rasheda.

"No. We can't keep getting together just to talk about Claire. It's getting to be like a wake every time we see each other. Are we a groups of friends, or are we just people who had someone in common? I mean, Lucy—remember?—we were friends before you even met Claire. I introduced you two."

Lucy's face burned; she felt humiliated. To calm herself, she studied the fraying sofa arm. It was beautiful, really, the rust-colored fabric worn down to a web of frail auburn threads. "It's just that the things we used to do together—cooking, gossiping about work, laughing at stories from the newspaper . . . You and I had a certain kind of . . . lightness. I don't have that any more."

Palms raised, Jane looked at the three of them in turn. "Maybe we can't go back. But we need to find new ways to operate."

Harry lifted his head. "I used to be jealous sometimes when Claire would exclude me and go off with her women friends. She told me that women love to be alone together." He turned to Rasheda. "Even straight women."

"And you men don't?" she replied.

"Well, we used to, but we don't make such a big deal of it any more."

Jane rolled her eyes. "No, you just reserve a few little clubhouses. Like the United States Senate."

He laughed. "We let a few of you in. But a guy's got to have something he can call his own. Anyway, now that I see what goes on during these girlfests, I'm glad I wasn't invited those other times. This is brutal."

"Jane, I think you're right," said Rasheda. "And wrong. We do need to consider the future. But the four of us were never a group. We were more like four planets that revolved around the same sun. It was only Claire that drew us together."

"So what happens to planets when their sun dies?" Jane asked.

"I don't know. Probably nothing pretty."

"Hey, isn't Kevin coming tomorrow?" Harry brightened. "Let's ask him. He's a science teacher."

The women exchanged glances. "Anyway," continued Rasheda, "the truth is—since we're playing that game—that I feel closer to you all now. I don't know if we're going to drift apart or what. But the four of us have been through something. No one else can ever know what that was like. And Lucy, I feel like you and I have a real friendship now, instead of just being Claire's daytime partner and her nighttime partner."

Lucy smiled. "That's a good way to describe it."

"Well, suppose we make a pledge," pressed Jane. "Once a year, no matter what's happening in our lives, the four of us will get together." She looked around. "All right?" The others nodded.

"And let's stop commemorating her death," proposed Rasheda. "I don't know why we'd want to honor that anniversary, especially considering when it falls. The Christmas season is supposed to be a celebration."

"I know," Lucy nodded. "I think dying at Christmas time was Claire's revenge for all those nights I made her watch *Miracle on 34th Street*."

"Let's meet on her birthday instead. May 8th, isn't it? Now, what would Claire want us to do in her memory?" wondered Rasheda.

Lucy and Harry turned to one another, eyebrows raised. "Eat," they replied in unison.

"By the time May rolls around, I'll be eating for two in earnest," Rasheda announced.

"Congratulations!" Lucy leaped up to give her a hug. "You've been wanting this for a long time, haven't you?"

"Long enough."

"That's good news," Jane chimed in. "Is Keisha excited?"

"She doesn't know yet."

"When will you tell her?" asked Harry.

"Not until I get good and big."

"So that's why you're not drinking tonight," he observed.

"You got it. But let's have a toast anyway, to my new baby and to our new plan." She lifted her empty glass.

"We're agreed, then," said Jane. "We'll gather in May, no matter what. But I'm serious about the other part. Everything can't be about Claire."

"Funny." Lucy gave a wan smile. "That's what I used to tell her."

Late that night, Lucy lay alone on the couch. The others were tucked into the three tiny bedrooms, their doors closed. She knew Claire would have sprayed the sofa with Lysol before she would sleep on it, but Lucy had been happy just to spread out her quilt and wrap it around herself. She reached behind her head to turn off the lamp, and the world vanished.

Fade to black, Claire might have said, although Lucy thought it was more of a plummet than a fade. Clouds covered the moon and stars, and even the lingering embers cast no light. The room was dark, as dark as—what? Sin? Gloom? Why did white people always associate darkness with evil, Lucy wondered. So many splendid things were black: Claire's wild hair; the generous earth; the long night, rich with whispers. No, Claire had not faded to black. She had faded, if anything, to white.

Claire had talked about colors as if they were objects that could be measured on a monitor and calibrated in degrees. It was all part of that terse TV language that Lucy would no longer hear. Crossfade. Dissolve. Split. Wipe. Now no one would stop a videotape at some perfectly ordinary moment and marvel, "Look at this transition!" No one would make Lucy watch a scene over and over until she *saw*: saw the layers of labor that constructed each weightless instant; saw the precision, the rigor, the balletic beauty of the filmmaker's invisible art. Lucy would watch movies now like everyone else, to see what happened next.

Her eyes had grown accustomed to the dark, but it was still unsettling. It made her regret she had buried Claire under the earth, without even a headstone for the first year, as the Jewish tradition required. Lucy would rather think of Claire's body as a plume of ash, gliding in the air somehow, maybe riding on a cloud.

A memory swept over her, vivid and immediate. She and Claire were leaving Chicago after the MLA conference, heading home. They held hands as the airplane lumbered down the runway and lifted with astonishing grace into the air. In the window seat, Lucy watched the earth fall away like a dropped plate. The plane dipped low over Chicago, the skyscrapers throwing blades of shadow across the lake. Claire was already dozing, her head on Lucy's shoulder, as they soared over fields of olive and tan and brown. Far below, a green river curled like a promise through the parched geometry of the Midwest.

That was the week Claire had bought her piece of land. And that week Lucy knew for a fact she was loved. Claire had no one else, no plans for escape. God knows what had been on Claire's mind, but it wasn't an ending.

Lucy hugged herself under the blue quilt she had brought from home. Her throat grew tight, but her eyes remained dry. She felt like one of the tiny luminous sparks she could still see in the fireplace, suddenly freed and floating skyward, into the night air.

Other Books from Third Side Press

NOVELS

On Lill Street by **Lynn Kanter.**   Margaret was a young, radical lesbian-feminist in the mid-1970s, her credentials unblemished, her ideals firm, when she moved to a mixed-gender house on Lill Street. $10.95   1-879427-07-9
  "Truly engrossing and a joyful experience."
                                                        —Bay Windows

Not So Much the Fall by **Kerry Hart.**   Through a fog of angst and chemically-induced confusion, on an odyssey from Memphis to Portland—and back again nine years later, Casey glimpses the consequences of her lifes actions.
  "Ultimately about life, and pain, and healing. . . . Not So Much the Fall *is up at the top of the 'must read' list."*
  —Alabama Forum

                                                $12.95   1-879427-24-9

AfterShocks by **Jess Wells.**   Tracy Giovanni had a list for everything, but when the Big One hit San Francisco—8.0 on the Richter scale—her orderly world crumbled.
                                                $9.95   1-879427-08-7
  "This book kept me up all night." —Kate Millet
  ALA 1993 Gay & Lesbian Book Award Nominee

The Sensual Thread by **Beatrice Stone.**   The simple story of Leah Kirby's awareness of the beings on earth around her and how that love transforms her sense of self. Being empathic gives making love a whole new dimension. $10.95   1-879427-18-4

Entwined by **Beatrice Stone.**   Determined to bring an old woman out of her years-long silence, Charly digs in to learn about Lottie every way she can. $10.95   1-879427-18-4
  "Intrigue, romance, wonder, searching, pain and finally, triumph. Guaranteed to slightly shift your sense of reality and help you to appreciate the power of dreaming."   —Amazon Bookstore News & Notes

Hawkwings by **Karen Lee Osborne.**   A novel of love, lust, and mystery, intertwining Emily Hawk's network of friends, her developing romance with Catherine, and the search throughout Chicago for the lover of a friend dying of AIDS.
                                                $9.95   1-879427-00-1
  ALA 1992 Gay & Lesbian Book Award Finalist

HEALTH BOOKS

Cancer as a Women's Issue: Scratching the Surface
Midge Stocker, editor.   Very personal stories explore how
cancer affects us as women, individually and collectively. Includes
multiple perspectives on dealing with breast cancer.
> *"If you are a woman, or if anyone you love is a woman,*
> *you should buy this book." —Outlines*
> *"An explicitly feminist perspective." —Sojourner*
> **Women/Cancer/Fear/Power series, volume 1**

$11.95   1-879427-02-8

Confronting Cancer, Constructing Change: New
Perspectives on Women and Cancer   **Midge Stocker,**
editor.   Confronting myths about cancer, presenting options for
responding to a cancer diagnosis, and provoking political action
to clean up the environment and reduce risks.
> *"Read it and reap." —Chicago Tribune*
> **Women/Cancer/Fear/Power series, volume 2**

$11.95   1-879427-09-5

Alternatives for Women with Endometriosis: A Guide by
Women for Women   **Ruth Carol, editor.**   Nutrition therapy,
acupuncture, chiropractic, biofeedback, and massage therapy are
a few of the available alternatives for relieving the pain of
endometriosis. $12.95   1-879427-12-5
> *"I highly recommend you read this book. It can open*
> *some new doors for you."*
> *—Endometriosis Association Newsletter*

To order any Third Side Press book or to receive a free catalog,
write to Third Side Press, 2250 W. Farragut, Chicago, IL
60625-1863. When ordering books, please include $2.50 shipping
for the first book and .50 for each additional book.

Third Side Press
because every issue has more than two sides.

The book you are holding is the product of work by an
independent women's book publishing company.